"Woven into this delicate story are themes echoing those of Bennett's first novel, *I Can Hear the Mourning Dove*. . . . Bennett's astute novel demonstrates enormous sensitivity."

— *Publishers Weekly*, starred review

". . . the dynamics between a thoughtful boy struggling to keep his unique spark alive and the oblivious public employees doing their best to quench it are poignantly realized. A sober portrait, with a conclusion . . . readers will find satisfying."

— *Kirkus Reviews*

". . . this is a measured, serious story and Floyd, not your stereotypical problem kid, is admirable in his devotion and application. . . . Readers puzzling out their own identities will empathize with . . . Floyd, fighting to define himself in a difficult world."

— *BCCB*, recommended review

". . . a fascinating story. . . ."   — *Times-Picayune*

"Fast paced and easy to read, this book reaches out and grabs the attention. . . ."

— *Sunday Advocate*

"... compelling..." — *School Library Journal*

"Floyd is finely drawn and comes painfully alive for the reader. ... The book is well written and certainly worth adding to a collection of ... literature."
— *VOYA*

"... in unfurling this unusual tale, author Bennett gives readers some genuine glimpses into what it's like to be a thoughtful teen trapped in a generally insensitive system."
— *New York Newsday / Los Angeles Times Book Review*

"... will appeal to students who liked *Tex* or *The Outsiders* by S. E. Hinton."
— *Book Report*, recommended review

An ALA Best Book for Reluctant Readers

DAKOTA
DREAM

POINT • SIGNATURE

DAKOTA DREAM

JAMES BENNETT

SCHOLASTIC INC.
New York Toronto London Auckland Sydney

No part of this publication may be reproduced in whole or in part, or stored in a retrieval system, or transmitted in any form or by any means, electronic, mechanical, photocopying, recording, or otherwise, without written permission of the publisher. For information regarding permission, write to Scholastic Inc., 555 Broadway, New York, NY 10012.

ISBN 0-590-46681-X

12 11 10 9 8 7 6 5 4 3 2 1   5 6 7 8 9/9 0/0

Printed in the U.S.A.   01

This book is dedicated to the memory of
Nancy Jeane Hansen, whose love for hung-out kids
was as big as the sea.

PROLOGUE

For the time being, you can call me Floyd.

Someday I will have my name legally changed to
Charly Black Crow. You can do that, but it's a lot
of hassle and it costs money, because you have to
go to court and fill out lots of legal forms, and all
that shit. Charly Black Crow is my chosen Sioux
name and after it's legally changed, that's the only
name I will answer to. Sometimes in school, especially in Mrs. Bluefish's class, I sign my papers
Charly Black Crow, AKA Floyd Rayfield. Whenever I
do it, Mrs. Bluefish comes unglued. This is not too
unusual for her, because she is a very excitable type,
and besides, she has this mistaken notion that I am
a troublemaker.

The thing you need to know first is that everything
in this story is true. I'm not making anything up,
I'm reporting everything exactly as it happened. I
thought about giving everybody fictitious names,
like they usually do in stories. To protect the innocent is the way it's usually put, I think. But then
I thought, *Why bother?* There's already so much work

1

that goes into writing a story, why put yourself through the extra hassle of thinking up a whole lot of fictitious names? Besides that, I never could quite figure out who were the innocent and who were the guilty. The real names just seemed a lot more on target than any names I could think up. If I ever get sued, it won't matter, because I will be living with the Indians and whatever happens in the white man's courts will not be any of my concern.

The second thing you need to understand is about my destiny to become an Indian. When I was a little kid, I didn't understand what a destiny was, and if you want the truth, I didn't understand much about Indians, either. All I knew was, I had a lot of admiration for Indians and I would always cheer for them to slaughter the cavalry whenever I watched a Western movie. What it came down to was, I wanted to be an Indian, the way other kids want to grow up to be a policeman or a fire fighter, or whatever.

Then one night last summer, I had this unbelievable experience where I saw a vision of myself as a Sioux warrior. The vision came to me in the usual way, in a dream. This is not the best time to go into the details, but to summarize the basics, the vision showed me that to become an Indian was not something for me to *want* or *not want*: It was my destiny.

In some ways, life gets easier once you understand your true destiny. Most of the time you know what to do, and you don't waste a lot of time wondering and worrying about your future. I would recommend to anyone that they should get in touch with their destiny.

Because I hold the ways of the Indian in such high esteem, I dye my hair black about once a month to get the red out, so my appearance will be more in touch with my Indian identity. All you have to do is use this brown liquid when you shampoo your hair, so there isn't much to it.

A couple of years ago, when I was still pretty much of a kid, I used to try to make my skin darker, too. It was pretty childish, but I don't hold it against myself, because when you're a little kid, you just naturally end up doing a few childish things. I never did find a satisfactory way to get my skin dark. I tried this tanning cream you can get at the drugstore, which is supposed to tan your skin even if you never go outside, but it made me look all blotchy like I had some kind of a disease. I tried mixing walnut husks in water and then rubbing the walnut water all over myself, which was a nice idea because it is an Indian ideal to use natural products at all times and live in true harmony with nature. But the result was, my skin got all streaked and I just looked dirty. Looking dirty is not for me.

I even tried laying out in the sun by the hour, but is that a boring pastime or what? I know girls who do it all the time, but you just lie there and nothing happens, except you get all sweaty, which means you attract all kinds of insects, so you just lie there with all this sweat and all these bugs. I gave that up after about one day.

Anyway, to get on with it, what this is is the story of how I ran away from home and became an Indian. Not just *joined* the Indians, you understand, but *became* an Indian. There's a big difference, which I intend to make clear eventually.

The hardest thing of all is knowing where to start. It always is. Think of any story about yourself that you might want to tell somebody, and you could practically start at the beginning of your whole life if you felt like it, because in a way, everything that ever happened to you has got something to do with what happens later on.

Oh, *Wakan Tanka*! Great Spirit.

Like I said, the hardest thing of all is knowing where to start . . .

CHAPTER ONE

It was the early part of the afternoon when I got to the Pine Ridge Reservation, exhausted from walking the motorcycle more than two miles and not getting much sleep for the past forty-eight hours. But I didn't pay much attention to the fatigue, because it was such a relief to finally be at my destination. I just went in through the main entrance.

Since it was the first part of June, there was lots of tourist activity. I was standing in the middle of a big, congested parking lot, surrounded by Delta 88s and Airstream campers and a whole lot of other barge-type vehicles favored by Mr. and Mrs. Tourist. I could see a lot of trailers and campers spread out like a settlement along the base of these very rugged foothills. There were a few Indians around, but more tourists.

This commercial part of the reservation was not likely to get me too excited. I happened to know from my research that the Pine Ridge Reservation covers many hundred square miles; this part was only the tip of the iceberg, and the tip was probably the least authentic part.

Besides that, it wasn't smart for me to just hang out in the public eye. As soon as I had my bearings, I walked the Kawasaki down a gravel path that led to a semiprimitive campground along the river. There were tipis you could rent and brick grills for cooking, and even a shower house made of cinder block. I found a private, wooded spot by the river where I could stash the bike and my backpack.

I felt so gritty from the trip I went up to the shower house and took a shower, even though I hadn't paid a camping fee and was probably a trespasser according to the letter of the law. I put on my clean clothes, which consisted of my spare T-shirt and blue jeans.

After that, I went back to my private spot by the river and mellowed out against the trunk of this big cottonwood tree. I was real hungry, but I was even more tired. There was no room in my head for the seized-up bike, or Carl Hartenbower's stolen car, or the cops, or Mrs. Bluefish, or Mr. Saberhagen, or Mrs. Grice, or anything that might be a problem. I didn't pay attention to my aches and pains.

The sky was bluer than you could imagine. It was the big sky, as the Indians called it. The river was sparkling like a crystal, and the rocky buttes on the other shore were like a picture frame. I felt like I had roots growing out of my body right into the ground. I was on the reservation, among the Dakota, and I had a peaceful, easy feeling, as that old song by The Eagles puts it. I was *in place*.

And then I was sound asleep.

What woke me up was the noise made by this guy in a pickup truck. He was collecting trash from the campsites and replacing garbage can liners.

I sat up and rubbed my eyes and looked at the low sun. The pickup truck was an old green GMC junker with PRR painted on the door; the guy was clearly an Indian. Now that I was at the reservation I needed to make contact, so I went on over and introduced myself.

It turned out his name was Donny Thunderbird, age nineteen. He wasn't very tall, but he was wiry, which is the ideal Indian physique.

"Where are you staying?" he asked.

I took him over to my private spot in the woods to show him.

"You don't have to stay here," he said. "A lot of the tipis are empty."

"What I'd like to find is a more or less permanent place to stay on the reservation. I don't think I could afford one of the tipis because my money would run out. I only started out with forty bucks."

"Are you on your own?"

"I'm on my own."

He asked me how old I was. I told him, "Actually, I prefer to think of myself as sixteen."

"You prefer?"

"Well, I haven't had my sixteenth birthday yet, but one time about a year ago, I read this story of these young German soldiers in World War One, and at the end of the book, the main character gets killed in battle. The way the author put it was, 'He fell, in the autumn of his twentieth year.' The thing was, he was really only nineteen, but if you think about it, once you've had your nineteenth birthday, you're living in your twentieth year, just like once you've had your first birthday, you're living in your second year. From the time I read that book, I got in the habit of thinking of myself as a year older."

Donny Thunderbird said, "You're only fifteen but you're on your own? What about your parents and your family?"

"I don't have any parents or family. That's a big part of the total picture." I could tell Donny was a guy I could trust, so I told him about taking off from the group home and coming 800 miles until I finally got here. I told him how I held the Indians in high esteem, especially the Dakota.

"You said you want a permanent place on the reservation," said Donny. "I don't understand what you mean."

"I'm hoping someone at the reservation will help me," I answered. I decided I might as well just get down to it. "I want to be a Dakota," I said. "As a matter of fact, it's my destiny to become one."

Donny looked at me for a few moments without saying anything. He didn't look at me the way I've been looked at before, like I was an alien, he just looked at me the way you look at a person when you're really concentrating. After this long silence, he asked me, "Is that your bike?"

Now it was my turn to hesitate. "You might say I'm borrowing it." Even though I could tell Donny Thunderbird was a guy to trust, there were limits.

"The bike is down," I added. "I had to push it all the way out here from town."

"That's more than a mile," he said.

"Don't I know it."

He wanted to know what was the matter with it, so I told him. "It's seized up. It was burning oil, but I was only driving at night so I couldn't see. There I was in the middle of Iowa with a seized-up bike. I couldn't drive it and I couldn't just leave it behind. I didn't know what I was going to do."

"So what happened?"

"I ran into this guy named Carl Hartenbower at a truck stop. He was on his way to Dry Gulch, Wyoming, to start a new job as a professional cowboy. Dry Gulch is a tourist town, and Carl was hired to sit on a chair in front of the general store and trading post all day long, and look like a cowboy of the Old West. Can you believe it, just sit there and get paid for it? He was perfect for it, though, he was a real leathery-looking kind of a guy. Anyway, he said we could tie the bike down on top of his car. It was a big Pontiac Bonneville. So that's what we did."

"And he brought you the rest of the way."

"As far as the edge of town. The rest was up to me. Carl was a weird guy. About a hundred miles back, he told me the car was stolen. That made me nervous, because being more or less on the run myself, I didn't like the idea of being in a car the cops were looking for. And it was pretty conspicuous with the bike tied on top. Of course, since the car wasn't his, he didn't care if the roof got scratched or dented."

"He does sound weird, but I'd say it was pretty lucky you ran into him."

Then I smiled. "You could call it luck, I guess. But the thing is, once you get in touch with your destiny, you get out of the habit of thinking of things as lucky breaks. Not to get overly philosophical, but that's what a destiny means: It's *supposed to happen*. That's how it's altogether different from lucky breaks or something you wish for."

Donny offered me a piece of gum, which I accepted. "You keep saying that, but I don't know how to take it. No offense."

"No problem. You're hearing all of this with an open mind. I appreciate that. What it comes down to is, I had a vision; it came to me in a dream. I'm destined to be a Dakota. I think I was a Dakota a hundred years ago, so it might be just a matter of returning. Sometimes the way to your destiny is through your previous lives."

Donny was quiet again, hearing it all. I liked the way I could tell him these things and not feel self-conscious. He finally said, "Are you hungry?"

"As a matter of fact I'm starved. The food in my backpack is all dried out."

"Hop in the truck. We'll go up to the snack bar."

The snack bar where Donny took me was part of the tourist area near that parking lot where I came in earlier. In addition to ordinary stores like a grocery store and a Laundromat, there were lots of gift shops and souvenir shops and trading posts, loaded with tourists. You could buy almost any kind of Indian merchandise, all of it authentic. With the tourists, the most popular stuff seemed to be items from the Southwest tribes, such as Navajo blankets, turquoise jewelry, and so forth. The best stuff from the Plains tribes were ceremonial pipes and certain weapons, such as shields made from buffalo hide, and very quality bows made out of bone.

I could have looked at the Indian merchandise for the rest of the evening, but I was too hungry. I got two chili dogs with onion and a large Pepsi. Before I knew it, we were back in the truck and driving along some gravel road through the timber, far away from the beaten path. I was wolfing my food and trying to get my bearings, but it was too dark by this time.

We must have gone two miles at least. Our destination turned out to be some maintenance buildings where equipment was kept, such as a tractor, a couple of dump trucks, mowers, et cetera.

Donny was throwing trash in a big Dumpster while I finished my food. We sat in a mechanic's shop where some old Indian men were playing cards, smoking cigarettes, and drinking whiskey. Even though it was just a maintenance shed, I felt privileged being in a place no tourists would ever see.

A very old Indian named Delbert Bear, who was one of Donny's distant great-uncles, was doing most of the talking. He smoked his pipe and told numerous stories of the glorious past when the warrior Dakota were the feared enemy of the white man's army. I asked Donny how old Delbert Bear actually was, and he said, "Nobody knows, including him."

Anyway, Delbert told of all the famous battles in great detail, such as when Crazy Horse defeated General Crook in the Battle of the Rosebud, and the terrible Dakota defeat at the hands of the Seventh Cavalry at Wounded Knee. I know for a fact that the defeat at Wounded Knee happened in 1890, so I asked Donny if Delbert Bear could really remember it.

Donny smiled and said, "Nobody knows, including him."

I had my journal with me, and I was making a point of writing down most of what came out of Delbert Bear's mouth. Donny asked me if I did a lot of writing and I told him I did. "I like to write stories," I said. "Sometimes I just write down notes and ideas for stories later on. I've been making notes on the Stone Boy legend for a long time."

"You probably know more about the Stone Boy legend than I do," he said.

I needed to be humble. I said, "There are different versions of the legend. I've sort of been working on a version which combines all the similar parts. You know, the essential stuff. There are gaps and missing pieces, stuff that's gotten lost over time. What I'd really like to do is fill in the gaps and still be authentic to the basic meaning of the legend. It's not easy."

Donny took a look at me before he answered. "A writer can do a lot of good for Indians."

I asked him how.

"I know a guy by the name of Chips," said Donny. "He's a Dakota on another reservation, but I've met him a couple of times. He publishes a newsletter twice a month on Indian civil rights and legal rights. People from all over the country subscribe to it, and I don't mean just Indians."

"Can you think of any more?"

"There's a guy in Minnesota I've never met. He writes columns on Indian history and traditions. His column is published in newspapers all over. There are also publications on Indian education and agriculture. That's what I'm interested in."

"What do you mean?" I asked.

"I just got done with my freshman year in junior college. I'm going to finish college and major in ag economics."

I said, "But aren't you happy now, doing what you're doing?"

"How do you mean?"

"Well," I said, "you've got your home, and your people, and your family. You have a job. You have your place."

Donny smiled. "A reservation is a place from the past. The Indian way of life is mostly history. It's good that there are people like Delbert, and reservations, so we don't forget the old ways. But Indians need help to live in the modern world."

That was a letdown for me, hearing him talk like that. Being on the reservation had me so mellowed out that I couldn't imagine finding anything wrong with it. As far as it being something out of the past, that was the best thing about it as far as I could see.

Donny Thunderbird went on. "I've got lots of other relatives up in the hills. They live the old ways. They still hoe the corn with elk antlers and they make arrows by rubbing sticks between two stones; the arrows get sold in the souvenir shops. But my people can't improve themselves by living the old ways, because the rest of the world doesn't live the old ways. One way that Indians need to become modern in is agriculture, and I've always been interested in crops and farming."

I was still a little uneasy about what he was saying, I guess because of my background of no home and no family and knowing what my destiny was. It didn't seem right somehow to take reservation life for granted. Maybe living on the reservation all your life, you didn't appreciate it quite as much. I wasn't about to argue with him, though, because you could tell he'd put a lot of thought into it. Besides that, he could have been treating me like I was wholesale weird, but he wasn't.

We changed the subject to my situation and what to do about it. "I'm not sure what advice to give you," Donny said.

"I understand your hesitation," I said. Which was true.

"It's just that no one ever came to me before and said he wanted to become a Dakota," he went on. "What we get here are tourists."

"It's not just that I *want* to become a Dakota," I reminded him. "It's my destiny."

"Right." he said. "I'm not forgetting. I'm probably going to have to talk it over with my uncle. He's the chief. Maybe he'll have some advice."

"Chief Bear-in-cave is your uncle?"

"How do you know his name?" Donny wanted to know.

"Didn't I tell you I've done research?"

He was smiling at me. "I guess you did. This gets better and better." Even though he was getting a grin out of it all, I knew he wasn't being disrespectful. I fully realized how fortunate I was to have him as my reservation contact; he could have been turning me in or calling the cops or something, but he wasn't, he was trying to help me.

"I'll take you back down to the campground," he said. "We'll find an empty tipi. It'll be on the house, no charge. You could use a night's sleep."

That was true. We drove on down and found an empty one. When he left, he said he'd see me in the morning.

I was too tired to move the bike, so I just left it stashed in the bushes. I brought my backpack to the tipi, looking at the sky full of stars and feeling mostly mellow. Then I stretched out on the tipi floor.

I felt somewhat bad about Barb, taking off on her like I did, and I felt some guilt about taking Nicky's bike. But he wouldn't miss it much; if it wasn't for me, it never would have been anything but down anyway. What I understood was, real important things, such as fulfilling your destiny, don't happen without a little pain. You can't make an omelette without breaking a few eggs. That's just the way the world works, so you have to accept it.

Then I fell sound asleep like a stone.

CHAPTER TWO

The next morning, I woke up real refreshed. After I got showered and brushed my teeth, I washed my dirty clothes right there in the shower house sink.

Shortly after that, Donny Thunderbird came by in the green pickup. He was throwing chunks of firewood on the ground in the campsites. He said Chief Bear-in-cave would be happy to talk to me.

"You mean right now?" I was a little surprised.

"You might as well, if you can. I gave him a little background, and he says he's not busy."

"Let's go, then."

I made sure I had my backpack with me when I got in the truck. I had some very unusual emotions on the way over, at least unusual for me. As a rule, I'm pretty good at sloughing off the emotional side of most situations, but to tell the truth, I was a little scared. In fact, more than a little. I wasn't scared of the *chief*, but it seemed like there might be a lot at stake. I've known for at least a year that it was my destiny to become an Indian, but if you got right down to it, it probably couldn't happen without the help of a tribal chief. This visit seemed like the crunch.

The chief lived in this ordinary trailer, around the curve of a foothill, no more than half a mile from the equipment shed and the mechanic shop.

Donny stopped the truck. I was sitting there in the passenger's seat, looking at the trailer but not moving. I guess I must have sat there for a while because Donny told me to go on in.

I got out of the truck. "Just go on in?" I said.

"Well, you know, knock first to be polite. But he's expecting you."

"Okay, then." I swallowed once, and Donny took off.

I walked up to the trailer and knocked on the door. The chief hollered to come in, so I went inside. It was dark because some of the curtains were drawn, and the trailer was on the west side of the hill. Chief Bear-in-cave was drinking coffee at the kitchen table. He asked me to sit down, so I sat on the other side of the table and put my backpack on the floor next to me.

I felt very humble being in the chief's presence, so I didn't want to stare; but I was taking in all his details. He was very old. His gray hair was in two long pigtails. His right eye was a cataract; it was milky white, so you could tell it was blind. When he talked or looked at you, he held his head sort of tipped to the side. His dark, leathery, creased skin gave him the look of nobility. He was wearing buckskin moccasins — just like mine — and blue jeans, a short-sleeved khaki shirt, and a Western-style belt. His only jewelry was a silver turquoise ring.

He wanted me to tell him about myself, so I told him basically what I had said to Donny Thunderbird the day before, about taking off from home and covering the 800 miles on Nicky's bike. I mentioned about the bike breaking down and getting a ride with Carl Hartenbower, but I didn't go into a lot of detail about that. I told the chief how I held the Indians in high esteem, especially the Dakota. I told him about all my reading of Indian literature, and my collection of Indian books.

He asked me my name, and I said: "Floyd Rayfield is my given name, but my preferred Dakota name is Charly Black Crow."

He didn't answer right away. That's one thing you learn about him: He never says anything right away. "Charly Black Crow is a good name," he finally said. Then he asked me about my home. "Who are your people?"

"I don't have any people," I answered, "not if you mean family. That's a big part of what this is all about. I never knew my parents; I've spent my life in foster homes and group homes."

"You live in one of these group homes now." He didn't say it like a question, but I knew that's what it was.

"Yeah," I said. "At least I did, up until three days ago. There's a housemother in charge, but she's a basic hairbag. I have a social worker I like better; she's real green, but she means well. I felt a little guilty taking off on her like I did, but I hope she'll understand — she knows how I'm always getting bounced around from one placement to another."

The chief took one of his long pauses. He got a pipe out of his shirt pocket, packed it, and lit it. I wondered at first if it was willow bark he was smoking, but I could smell right away it was some kind of cherry tobacco. After he took several puffs, he said quietly, "Your love for the Dakota is plain. Is there something I can do for you?"

I couldn't see any reason to beat around the bush, not after I'd come this far and so much was on the line. I took a deep breath and said, "I want to live here on the reservation. As a matter of fact, I want to become a Dakota."

He was still listening, so I went on: "The truth is, it's not just something I *want*. It's my destiny to become a Dakota."

"Can you explain what you mean by destiny?" he wanted to know.

I said, "Your destiny is what you were meant for. You have to find a way to fulfill it or else you will live your life in frustration. The things that try and block you from your destiny you have to have the courage to ignore, and put yourself in a position to fulfill it. That's why I'm here."

"And how did you learn this destiny?"

"The usual way," I said. "I had a vision that came to me in a dream."

"I would like to hear about the dream, if you don't mind," said the chief.

"Of course." I felt truly honored, the way he was treating me with such sincerity and respect. "I had the dream about a year ago. All the details were really crisp to me, like things in a photograph. In the dream, I was a Dakota warrior on horseback. It was in the middle of a winter night, the Moon of Popping Trees, one brave called it. I was one of twenty or thirty braves riding single file on a narrow path in a dense forest. It was a crystal-clear night of a million stars and a full moon, but the snow was deep, so our progress was slow."

"All of you," said Chief Bear-in-cave. "Where were you headed?"

"That's the worst part. We didn't know. We were retreating from a minor battle with soldiers at a place called Willow Creek. One of the Indians, whose name was High Horse, had a bullet lodged in his hip; every once in a while he would groan or cry out with pain.

"The winter had been tragic already and there was a lot of it left. The herds were gone, and cattle were scarce. The soldiers had forced us off our lands and out of our camps. Maybe we'd go to one of the settlements; all we knew for sure was, we were freezing and starving."

The chief's eyes were half closed, but I knew he was hearing every word. I could have added more details, but it seemed better to keep my summary brief. He didn't seem ready to speak, so I wrapped it up: "My mind was one with the other warriors. It was wholesale despair; it was freezing, and starving, and defeat, and pain. But the thing that was worst of all was having no home to return to. The soldiers had taken everything, so there was no place left to call home. When I woke up, I understood my destiny. The reason I respected the Indians so much, and wanted to become one, was because I must have been a Plains Indian in a previous existence. When I fulfill my destiny to become a Dakota, it will just mean returning to my true nature."

Then I stopped talking. My cards were on the table, as honest as I could be. I waited for the chief.

He finally said, "Thank you. It is good of you to share all of this." Then he had to stop to relight his pipe. When he had it going, he said, "Now I have another question. What is it you admire most about the Dakota?"

I had to think a minute. If I tried to tell him everything I admired about Dakota ways, it would take too long; I needed to summarize the basics. "Belonging is important," I said. "Real important. When I was talking to Donny Thunderbird, he told me about his relatives all over the reservation. He has cousins with no mother or father, but because they are members of the tribe, they will never be without a home. They will always belong to something.

"Also, the Dakota way is a way of harmony, especially harmony with nature. The buffalo kill is not just slaughtering some creature to eat. Somehow it seems like oneness, but I don't know if that's the best word for it. Black Elk said, 'Is not the earth a mother and the sky a father?' Now I'm just rambling; my thoughts aren't really organized."

"Your thoughts are good thoughts," said the chief. He took another pause, and I could tell the wheels in his brain were really turning. Then he raised an index finger up next to his head and said, "I have a story."

Chief Bear-in-cave told me the story of a brave named Two-Claw. When he was a young man, Two-Claw captured a bear and tamed it. He got it so tame that he turned it more or less into a household pet. After a long time passed, Two-Claw didn't want to be bothered with the bear anymore, and it was then that he realized his dilemma: He couldn't release the bear into the wilderness, because it wouldn't be able to survive on its own.

People in the tribe told Two-Claw that the only thing to do was kill the bear because it would be better off dead than living helpless in the wilderness. Two-Claw had a lot of honor; he understood the wisdom of this advice, and he cursed himself for playing a game that turned a bear into something unnatural. He told the people in his tribe that he was going to kill the bear, so he took it up into the hills.

When Two-Claw got high up in the hills and far away from anybody, he couldn't do it. He couldn't bring himself to kill the bear. So he hid the bear in this cave, where it would be safe. To keep it safe, he had to return quite often with food and to check for predators. He had to carry the burden of this chore for many years, because the bear was young, and he also had to carry a burden of extreme humility because his situation was a constant reminder of how he had meddled with the ways of nature.

When Chief Bear-in-cave was done with this story, he looked straight at me with his one good eye and said, "It's a lot like that when you're an Indian on a reservation."

Well, I have a lot of appreciation for stories, and I felt honored that the chief took the time to tell me the Two-Claw adventure. But I wasn't sure I understood the underlying meaning of the story. Or maybe the truth was, with this sort of creeping disappointment I felt in the pit of my stomach, I understood better than I wanted to.

There wasn't time to think about it then. The chief got out of his chair and went into the den part of the trailer, where there were a whole lot of books in bookcases, all dusty and disorganized-looking.

When he came back to the table, he had an index card and a ballpoint pen. He said to me, "I don't think you want to give me the name of that housemother of yours, but please write down the name and address of that social worker."

Naturally, this request didn't exactly make me comfortable. I had thought the chief and I were really into each other here. What was he going to do now, turn me in? While I was staring at the blank card, the chief was sitting down again.

"Are you going to call my social worker?" I asked. He was smiling at me. "I don't know. I have to think a while, until I know the right thing."

"I don't understand."

He still had the smile. He still had both of his front teeth, but only one molar, as far as I could see. He said, "Dakota teaching says that if you have any wisdom, you know when it's time to do a thing. Even death; you know when it's time to go off for dying. So please write, and I will wait for wisdom."

I decided all I could do was trust him. I had come this far, hadn't I? I wrote Barb's name and address on the card and I even added her phone number. I pushed the card across the table.

"Thank you," said Chief Bear-in-cave. I watched him fold the card and put it in his shirt pocket, right behind his eyeglasses. Then he said, "Now I have a suggestion. I think it's time for your *hanblecheya*."

This didn't sink in for a few moments, maybe because I was still thinking about the index card. Did he say *hanblecheya*?

The chief asked did I hear him.

"Yeah, I did. Sorry."

"If you go on the *hanblecheya* with your heart and mind open, your direction will become clearer. Your wisdom will increase."

He was talking about the sacred tradition of the vision quest. The *hanblecheya* meant four days and nights fasting in the wilderness, seeking enlightenment. I could hardly believe it. In the Dakota tradition, it was holy; the chief's offer meant respect and honor.

Chief Bear-in-cave asked me if I understood the tradition of the *hanblecheya*.

"Of course," I answered. "Maybe not every single detail." I summarized quickly my knowledge of the vision quest tradition, and the chief was satisfied.

"*Hanblecheya* is hard," warned the chief. "Very hard. Do you feel yourself ready?"

"When would I go?"

"Today." He was looking at his watch. "Donny Thunderbird will be in charge of your preparations."

"What do I do to get ready?" All of a sudden it seemed like things were going so fast.

The chief was on his feet. "Donny will guide you through your preparations. If you change your mind, if you decide not to go, there's no shame."

We were shaking hands. Before I knew it, I was out the door, heading along the gravel path in the direction of the campground. My mind was spinning so fast, I didn't even notice my surroundings. I was a runaway with a stolen bike; there might be cops after me, but Chief Bear-in-cave was making me an offer of utmost respect. I had made the 800-mile journey of hardships, but now my destiny seemed at hand. The *hanblecheya* filled me with hope, but also with fear. Besides, there was the index card and the disappointing story of Two-Claw's tame bear. What about that?

There was too much to think about, so it seemed like a good idea to let the numbness take over. I listened to the gravel crunching beneath my feet.

When I got to the campground, I found Donny cleaning the shower house. As soon as I summed up my conversation with Chief Bear-in-cave, he nodded and said, "We need to get started with the preparations."

I helped him load some trash bags into the bed of the pickup. He suggested we ought to move my bike to a safer place. "What if we take it up to the equipment shed?" he asked.

"That sounds like a good idea," I said. "I'd feel better if it's not in the bushes."

We muscled it up into the truck, and Donny got a good look at its run-down condition. "I'm surprised you got here on this thing," he said.

"I didn't, remember? It broke down on the way. If you think it's bad now, you should've seen it before we worked on it." But my mind wasn't really on the bike; I was still more or less numb from being on the threshold of an authentic *hanblecheya*.

After we dumped the trash, we put the bike in a woodshed, next to a snowplow. The next thing I knew, we were back in the truck and heading up into the hills. Donny was maneuvering the truck at a fairly high speed on about the most primitive dirt and gravel road I'd ever seen.

He asked me if I was scared.

"I'm scared," I said. "If I start now, when will I be finished?"

"This is Wednesday, and we should get you

started by noon. You'll be finished at noon on Sunday."

"Is it okay if I take my backpack?"

"Sure, you can take it. I'll fix you a canteen of water, too. Since the *hanblecheya* is a fast, you can't have any food, but you can have water. In the old days, you couldn't even have water, and some people actually died on their vision seek."

We were gaining altitude. I don't know how many miles we were actually covering, probably not as many as it felt like, but we were a long way from anything that had to do with tourists. There were scattered clusters of pine forest, but mostly rocks and brush. I saw a few patches of puny-looking corn, maybe ankle high; in one of the patches, some women were hoeing.

"What if I chicken out?" I asked. I had to know.

"You thinking of backing out?"

"No, I mean what if I can't hack it? What if I give up after a day or two and quit?"

"There's no shame in that. It's not unusual."

If you say so, I thought to myself. We came to a plateau clearing, where there was a group of twenty or twenty-five tipis and a store that didn't look like a store; it looked like a small warehouse made of logs and mud.

Donny parked the truck and said with a big smile, "My hometown."

If it was a town, it wasn't one that would show up on anybody's map. What it really was, was a trip back in time to another world. Donny spent a few minutes talking to some guys in front of the store. One of the men was Delbert Bear, but I didn't recognize the others. After that, Donny took me to a tipi that belonged to his older sister, Kaia, and her husband, Gilbert. Gilbert wasn't there because he was away on some highway construction job.

This was not a canvas tipi; it was made of real buffalo hides. It did have a couple of modern features, such as cots to sleep on, and instead of an ordinary fireplace in the center, it had a wood-burning stove, with an exhaust pipe that went straight up through the top. The water, which had to be fetched from a well, was stored in large metal army cans; I tried lifting a full one, but it felt like it weighed about a thousand pounds.

"You need to eat," Donny told me. "You're looking at four days without any food."

He no more than got the words out of his mouth than Kaia showed up with a cast-iron skillet full of casserole. She gave us both a heaping serving on metal plates that looked like they came from an old GI field kit. I took a few bites and said, "I hate to put your sister to this trouble. I could have bought some hot dogs or hamburgers at the snack bar; it's not like I don't have any money."

Donny was shoveling it in. "You can't eat that crap now, you're going on a vision seek. You need Dakota food."

"What is this stuff?"

"Chicken and eggplant fried in corn meal."

"It's good," I said. Which was true, but I didn't

have my usual appetite, not with all the butterflies I felt in my stomach. I asked Donny what would be next, after we finished eating.

"Delbert is going to come. He was a shaman, a long time ago. You'll be spending a couple of hours in the sweat lodge for purification."

"Was he a real shaman?" I asked. "Or does he just think he was?"

Donny smiled. "He was a real shaman."

"There are so many people putting themselves out for me. It's very humbling."

"Humility is the right frame of mind for vision seeking."

"But I don't feel worthy."

"I believe in your sincerity," said Donny. "So does the chief, or he wouldn't be recommending the *hanblecheya*. My advice is, don't think."

"Have you gone on the *hanblecheya*?" I asked him.

He was finishing off his food. He nodded his head. "I did go once, two years ago. Four days is a long time to go with no TV or stereo or books or other people. It can really grind on you. The worst mistake is to think too much or try to figure things out."

"But aren't you supposed to learn your vision?"

"You're supposed to *receive* your vision. You can't make it happen, you have to let go."

I told him, "When I left the chief's trailer, I felt my brain spinning around with questions. It was too much. I felt myself wanting to go into a numb-out. I think I should just let myself go into that head."

"That's exactly it. Just let it go." Then he said if I was done eating, we'd better get started. I told him I needed to go to the bathroom, and I'd also like to have a little willow bark for my pipe. He showed me the way to the outhouse, then he headed for that store down at the end of the clearing to get the willow bark.

The outhouse turned out to be a two-holer, although I couldn't figure out why. I was sitting there over one hole looking at the extra and wondering would you take a crap with someone side by side? This thought made me giggle, and then I started laughing out loud.

When I got back to the tipi, Donny and Delbert Bear were waiting. They both had blue jeans on, but no shirt. Delbert was also wearing an authentic Dakota headdress made of eagle feathers.

Delbert had a small dish of blue paint that looked like greasepaint. He used his thumbs to put the paint on both sides of his nose and under his eyes. Then he did the same to Donny and to me. Delbert's ancient skin was like loose leather. He smelled like whiskey, but I reminded myself you don't judge people by what's on the surface.

Donny gave me about half a dozen plastic pouches of shredded willow bark, which I put in my backpack. He also gave me a large metal canteen full of water. It looked like shirts were out of touch, so I took mine off and put it in the backpack, too.

To get to the sweat lodge, we had to follow a path through a small section of timber, mostly pine. Since

Delbert was leading the way, we weren't walking very fast. He was carrying a bundle of sage and lighting pieces of it along the way. He was chanting as he went, but it sounded more like mumbling; I guess at his age, there's not much difference. The only words I could make out were *Wakan Tanka*, the Great Spirit, and *Inipi*, which means purification rite.

Donny told me that he didn't understand every single word Delbert Bear was saying, but basically he was appealing to *Wakan Tanka* so that my purification rite would be a good one. "Sweating in the lodge will purify your body," said Donny. "But it will take *Wakan Tanka* to purify your soul."

This was all stuff I knew from reading about it, but I felt so honored and privileged, I was getting a head rush. There was Delbert's prayer and the smell of the burning sage and the pine limbs overhead with the background of the blue sky. Was this authentic or what? If Mrs. Bluefish or Mr. Saberhagen or Mrs. Grice could see me now, they'd be laughing out of the other sides of their faces.

We came to a clearing where a couple of women were putting the final touches on getting the sweat lodge ready by throwing extra buffalo hides over it. It was a small structure in the shape of a dome, built out of willow saplings. "The sweat lodge is not always ready," Donny explained, "because *hanble-cheyas* are not that common anymore."

I didn't know where the two women disappeared to, but all of a sudden it was just Donny and Delbert and me in front of the lodge. Still chanting, Delbert held up burning sage to the north, south, east, and west. I didn't need Donny to tell me — Delbert was offering the prayer of sage to the four corners of the universe; there was no limit to the domain of *Wakan Tanka*. Delbert Bear kept burning the sage and offering it to the four corners so many times, I began to wonder if he was losing his concentration. But when he finally pulled back the flap, I didn't need any instructions; I knew it was time for me to enter.

Inside, the lodge was dark and hot. Hot as hell, in fact. Because the sides were so sloped, there was only room at the center to stand up straight. The buffalo hides left a few small gaps, so there was some light coming through, but not much.

Delbert and Donny were still on the outside, with the flap pulled halfway. Delbert was saying something to me in Dakota.

"What's he saying?" I asked Donny.

"He said you need to get naked now."

I wasn't sure I heard it right, so I asked him to repeat it; there was already sweat popping out on my forehead and my temples.

"The tradition is to go through *Inipi* without any clothes on. Besides the fact that it frees all your pores, it symbolizes leaving the things of the world behind."

This was the unexpected. Maybe along the way I'd skipped a chapter I should have read. I was a little self-conscious, especially with the two of them standing there looking at me. I finally said, "It sounds logical, but would you mind closing the flap and I'll just throw my clothes out?"

They closed the flap, which made the hut real, real dark, which made it easier for me to take off my clothes. I tried not to think about what I was doing.

I heard Donny's voice from the outside: "You'll be glad you're not wearing any clothes. You'll be sweating so hard, clothes would just make you miserable."

I rolled up my blue jeans, moccasins, and underwear and pitched them outside. I could hear Donny say, "I'll put these in your backpack. We'll be back in a couple of hours. Are you okay in there?"

After a few moments I said, "I'm okay."

After a few moments' pause of his own, I heard Donny say, "Don't think."

Then I heard their footsteps fade and I knew they were gone. I turned around. Even though this was real Dakota ritual, the authentic *Inipi*, and I felt real honored, I also felt real weird. I was standing there naked, in this semidark hut of a sweat lodge, in a different world. There was all this heat and so much silence, you could practically hear it.

It didn't take long for my eyes to adjust, though. In the center of the dirt floor there was a big hole, not deep but about three feet across. In the hole there were a dozen or so big rocks, some of them bigger than a volleyball. They were all pretty smooth and rounded, which told me they were probably meant only for this ritual purpose. Besides having a nice shape, they were hot. When I sat down on the folded blanket next to the circle, I found out how hot. It was like sitting beside a fireplace. I didn't know who had heated the rocks, but I figured it must have been Delbert, and maybe he had some help. A small amount of steam was rising from the hot rocks, and I wondered what caused it.

By the time I got myself into a more or less comfortable position by folding my legs, the sweat was pouring out of me. It was running down my face and chest in little streams, which was uncomfortable; it was also gratifying when I remembered the purpose. According to Dakota belief, the water spirits rid the body of impurities so there's no block in communication with *Wakan Tanka*. If your *hanble-cheya* was going to be a success, you had to get rid of your impurities. I wondered if I could stand this flow of sweat for two hours, but I knew that kind of thought was dangerous; you had to do what you had to do. This was destiny here.

The vapor coming from the rocks smelled a little bit like sage, and it was also sort of hypnotic. After a while I found myself going into a mild numb-out.

Then the woman came in, carrying a pitcher.

It was one of the two women I had seen earlier, draping up the buffalo hides. She leaned down next to me and started sprinkling water from the pitcher onto the rocks. There was plenty of hissing and steam came rising up; the smell of sage was real strong, so I guess there was some of it mixed in with the water.

Real quick, I flinched and sat up straight. I was sitting there naked, and this woman was doing chores next to me. I could feel myself turning red as a beet, though I doubted she could notice that, not in that much darkness, in a cloud of rising steam. To tell the truth, though, she didn't pay any attention to me at all. After she sprinkled the water for a few seconds, she was gone.

Even for a few minutes after she left, I still had the aftermath of being embarrassed, which meant my skin had a burning sensation added to the sweat flow. What the hell, I thought to myself, she was just a woman doing her job; I was getting exactly the same treatment as any young Dakota man going through *Inipi*.

The rest of the time seemed to go pretty fast. It was so hot and stifling, I had trouble breathing, but I got back into the numb zone and pretty much stayed in it. Every once in a while I wiped the sweat off my face so it wouldn't bother my breathing. When the woman came a second time with her water pitcher, it didn't make me uncomfortable. She came and went like it was a dream.

The next thing I knew, Delbert Bear and Donny were at the flap, asking me if I was ready to come out.

When I stepped out, the sun was so blinding, it took me several minutes to get my eyes adjusted. The breeze felt cool to me, even though it was a warm summer day. I was standing there in the altogether, shivering in the chill of gooseflesh, with all my sweat running down to the ground.

Donny asked me how it went.

"Pretty good, I think. The time went fast."

"You can use some of the sage to dry off."

"My impurities must be gone," I said. "It's like all my fluids are emptied."

Donny put the canteen in my hand. "Have a drink," he said.

I took a few swallows from the canteen, which was a big-time relief. I had to keep my eyes mostly closed because the light was still so blinding. I started wiping the sweat with the clusters of sage, which was not real comfortable. The sage is real holy to the Dakota, and real important to any ritual, but it's not very absorbent. It did knock off some of the water, and besides that the sun was drying me off, too.

By the time I got myself mostly dry, and had my blue jeans and my moccasins back on, Delbert Bear was lighting a ceremonial pipe. It was a real Sioux ceremonial, about three feet long, nearly twice as long as my own pipe. The three of us passed the pipe, taking turns smoking it. Since I don't inhale when I use a pipe, I couldn't tell for sure what was in the bowl; all I know is, it didn't taste like willow bark. No Dakota ritual is complete without the passing of the sacred pipe; we smoked it all the way down until it was out.

Then Delbert took some more sage pieces from his bundle and burned to the four corners once more.

"It's time now," said Donny. "Are you ready?"

I had this feeling of being lifted above ordinary stuff. I guess that's what being purified means, but it's hard to find the words to express a thing like that. I said to Donny, "I'm ready."

We had to walk through some more woods until we came out on a huge prairie that sloped upward a long way into the distance. On the far side of the rise, at its highest point, there was a mound with a heavy growth of prairie grass and high weeds. The mound seemed to have a slit in it, but it was too far away to make out much. Just on the back side of the mound, there were a few boulders and a cluster of pine trees.

"What's up there?" I asked Donny.

"It's a cave. The opening is bigger than it looks from here."

"It's the place for *hanblecheya*," I said reverently.

"It's *a* place. It's a traditional one. I recommend it, but any place would work as long as you're off by yourself and your mind is open. It's not the place that matters, it's what's inside you that really counts."

"Is it the site you used?"

"Yes."

"I'm sure it will be just fine." I didn't tell him I was getting scared again.

It took us a while to get there. It was several hundred yards and even though the slope was gentle, we went by Delbert's pace. He stopped every once in a while to catch his breath and burn some sage.

When we finally got to the mound, I found out

how big it truly was; the opening itself, which looked
so small from a distance, was big enough to walk
through without touching. The cave inside was big,
big as an average-sized bedroom, I would say. It was
dark and moist, and cooler than the air outside.

Delbert Bear began chanting again and burning
sage to the four corners. Donny took me up above
where there was a small clearing among the group
of pine trees, a nice cushion of pine needles on the
ground. We were on a high spot, so the view was
sensational in all directions. The clearing seemed like
such a mellow place, I asked Donny if I had to spend
the whole *hanblecheya* in the cave, or was it okay to
come up here?

"You can be where you want to be," he said.
"According to Delbert and the other old-timers,
when Black Elk went vision seeking he came here.
He spent most of his time pacing and smoking his
pipe."

It was truly awesome to think that the Dakota
were putting me on the very spot used by Black Elk
himself. "Is it really true?" I asked him.

He smiled. "I don't know for sure, but I like to
think it's true."

We climbed back down to the cave opening; some
of the prairie grass was so tall, you had to push it
out of your face. I guess Delbert Bear must have
been getting weary, because he went ahead and
burned up all the sage left in his bundle.

Then Donny said it was time for them to leave.
He gave me the Dakota embrace, where you grip

the back of each others' upper arms. So did Delbert.

"Good luck, good vision," said Donny.

I told him thanks. I was scared again, and I guess afraid what words might come out.

"If you have to come back early, you'll be able to find the village, right?"

I licked my lips. "I could find it, no problem. But I don't intend for that to happen."

"Good." He smiled again.

Then Delbert said something long to me in Dakota, but the only words I could understand were *Wakan Tanka* and *Hanblecheya*. I could tell it was some kind of a blessing. I nodded my head and said, "Thank you."

After that, when they started to leave, he said something else to me, but I couldn't understand any of his words. Donny said, "He's reminding you to get naked. Clothes are things of the world."

"Do I have to do it right now?"

He laughed. "You can wait."

Then the two of them were headed down the hillside. I just stood there for the longest time, watching them get smaller and smaller. I could see clear to the woods we had come through, and way beyond that. As a matter of fact, I could've seen all the way to Chief Bear-in-cave's trailer, except there was a mountain blocking it. But it was a radical thought to realize I could see six or seven miles in any direction. It was pretty obvious why this was considered an ideal spot for vision seeking.

I stood there watching until Delbert and Donny

were just specks and I realized I wouldn't be able to make them out when they went into the woods.

Now that I was all alone, it felt like it was just me and the universe. I wasn't sure what to do, but then I remembered not to think too much. I went inside the cave to check it out better. Even though it was large, most of the ceiling was too low to stand up straight. The roomiest part was close to the entrance, which was also the part with the strongest light.

There were several sage branches scattered on the dirt floor, probably used in the past by Dakota vision seekers for sleeping on. It seemed like a comfortable idea, besides giving me the good feeling of a history link; I gathered the sage together to form a makeshift bed. Right next to it, I emptied my backpack and laid out my things side by side. My blue jeans and my two T-shirts. My ceremonial pipe. My journal and two Bic pens. Toothbrush, soap, and washcloth. The denim jacket. I decided the jacket would make a good pillow, so I rolled it up and laid it on the sage. The light from the opening was good once your eyes got adjusted, because the opening faced south. But I knew when the sun went down, the cave would be completely dark.

I remembered then about leaving all the things of the world behind, and I took off my moccasins and my blue jeans. I decided to go up and sit under the pine trees, so I picked up my pipe and my journal. At the entrance I hesitated because I was about to go out naked, but then I realized that was foolish because who would look at me? There wasn't a soul for miles.

After I got up there, it took me a few moments to find a comfortable seat. Pine needles make a nice cushion underfoot, but your bare ass isn't as tough as your feet. I either got myself comfortable or I got used to it; anyway, I packed my pipe with some of the willow bark and lit up.

It was almost completely silent, except for a few birds high up in the pines. As far as I could see in any direction, there was the rugged terrain of the Black Hills, mountains, valleys, and prairies. This could have been a hundred years ago or a thousand.

Somewhere out there was the Little Bighorn, and the Rosebud, and Wounded Knee. How many hundreds of years of Sioux history? I was sitting on the spot where Black Elk himself once came for vision seeking. Maybe more than once. When I got into the *hanblecheya* head, the right zone for visions, maybe the spirit of Black Elk would visit me. Maybe I would make contact with my former self, the warrior from the dream who was riding from Willow Creek. *Maybe a lot of things, when it comes to your destiny*, I told myself.

The whole experience was giving me a big-time head rush. The best thing of all, probably the most important thing, was that I *belonged* here. I wasn't sneaking or pretending, I was only twenty-four hours on the reservation, but it didn't get any more authentic than this. This was my *hanblecheya*, on ancient, holy ground, directed by Chief Bear-in-cave himself.

As soon as the pipe was smoked out, I opened up my journal. Anything as major as my own vision quest should be written down, and here I was looking at four days' free time with no distractions. There ought to be enough time to receive my vision and also write out all the notes I wanted.

I thumbed past my story contest entry, the one called "Mask," which had freaked Mrs. Bluefish out, and then I flipped by some of my notes on the Stone Boy legend. When I got to a fresh page, I wrote *hanblecheya* across the top.

I sat there thinking for a while, and then decided to go right on back in time to that day in April when I moved into Gates House.

CHAPTER
THREE

Since I'd never been to Joliet before, I didn't recognize any of the city landmarks, but Gates House looked familiar, anyway. It looked just like most of the dipshit places that are run by social services anywhere you go. It was a dull brick rectangle, with no porch and a few small windows. Not old, but real tacky. It looked like it didn't belong in the neighborhood. There was a parking lot in front, but no trees.

Leonard, my social worker from Peoria, was driving me. He helped me get my stuff inside and then he introduced me to Mrs. Grice, who was the supervisor of the house. She was short and dumpy and old, with no upper teeth.

She started showing me and Leonard around, beginning with the dining room and lounge, which were close to the front door. I really didn't need this guided tour because I knew exactly where everything would be; besides which, Mrs. Grice had this annoying habit of popping her loose lip back and forth.

When she showed us my room I was glad to find it was at the end of the hall, next to the fire escape. That always feels like a good location, but I don't know why. The room was empty and smelled like paint. There was one small window, fairly high up.

"This room's been empty for a couple of weeks," Mrs. Grice said, "so we've had it cleaned and painted. Both beds are empty, so you can choose either one. We expect a roommate soon, but some of his material is being processed, so we don't know exactly how soon."

I didn't say anything.

She said, "You may decorate your half of the room if you like with pictures or posters, but I don't allow any vulgar material. And you're not to make marks on the walls or deface them in any way." She was looking at me and popping her lip again. I didn't say anything.

She showed me some more stuff around the house, I can't remember what all, and then Leonard said it was time for him to hit the road. We said good-bye, and he wished me good luck. It wasn't exactly an emotional farewell, since I'd only known him a couple of months. That's the way it is in social services, they come and they go. High turnover is how it's usually put. It's probably good that that's the way it is, because the worst mistake you could make in the system would be to get attached to someone.

After Leonard was gone, Mrs. Grice put on these Scrooge glasses and started reading all the rules you had to go by when you live in Gates House. Since it was just me now, the polite tone was gone out of her voice, but I didn't care. I knew all about group home rules and which ones you had to watch out for.

She showed me the bulletin board between the dining room and the lounge. "You need to check it every day," she said, "for announcements, work schedules, and so on. If a resident is put on probation for any reason, it's posted here."

I spoke for the first time: "I've never been on probation in my life."

She looked at me over the top of her glasses before she answered. "Good. Let's keep it that way, shall we?"

When she was done with the rules and procedures, I told her I'd like to take a walk.

"You may, if you use the sign-up sheet. You need to write your name, the time, your destination, and the time you're going to return."

"How can I write a destination if I don't have one?"

Again, she looked at me over the top of her glasses. "Are you using a tone with me?"

"No tone at all," I said.

"Because one thing I've noticed with youngsters over the years, where you find a tone of voice you usually find an attitude problem."

"I'm not using a tone," I said again. "But I've never been to Joliet before, so I wouldn't know what to put for a destination."

She pushed her glasses back up. "Just for this

time, you may write that you're taking a walk." She looked at her watch and added, "Make sure you're back no later than two. Your social worker called and said she might come by later this afternoon."

That was about all the time I wanted to spend one on one with Mrs. Grice, so the walk was a relief. The neighborhood was a little uneven, with some of the houses kept up nice but others run down. After three blocks I came to a big park called Vale Park, which had a few hills and a stream and lots of old shade trees. I sat under one of the trees for a while, just glad to be off by myself. I thought about Mr. and Mrs. Gibbs; I probably wouldn't be seeing them again.

As soon as I got back to Gates House, I went straight to my room to unpack my stuff. There was a guy there, sitting on the other bed, the one I didn't plan to use. He said his name was Greg Kinderhook. I asked him if he was going to be my roommate. "No," he said. "They're holding this open for Nicky. He's been in Gates House before, but not lately."

I took a good look at Kinderhook, who was wearing a pair of khaki walking shorts and a Hawaiian shirt. He reminded me of the Pillsbury dough boy. His skin was white as chalk, and he was pudgy, but all his fat was slack. It was loose fat, like all he had was bones with fat attached.

I opened up one of my suitcases and started putting some clothes away in one of the dresser drawers. I asked Kinderhook why he wasn't in school.

"I had a doctor's appointment, so I got out early. I have gastrointestinal problems."

I took another look at him. Even his knees and elbows were loose fat; I'd never seen a body quite like it. I felt like telling him some exercise and a little muscle tone would be good for him, but what would be the point?

He asked if he could sit there and talk to me while I unpacked my stuff. I shrugged my shoulders and said, "If you want to."

I started unpacking more stuff, and Kinderhook started in with the questions. "Where are you from?"

"I've been living in a foster home downstate," I said.

"How come they took you out?"

"The lady got sick. They couldn't be foster parents anymore."

"What was she sick with?"

"Diabetes," I said. Then I stood up straight. "Kinderhook, I said you could sit here, but you can kiss off the twenty questions."

"Sorry," he said.

The thing is, I knew exactly what he was up to. In group homes there are alliances. These sort of pecking orders are established, just like you find in any institutional residence. Since I was new, and since he was out of school early, he was taking the opportunity to get a jump on finding out how I might fit in, and whether I was somebody whose good side he should be on.

He changed the subject back to the guy named

Nicky, my future roommate. "He's been living with his mother, but it looks like they're going to pull him out."

I didn't say anything.

"He's hung out while they have staffings on him."

"I figured." I said. I've been hung out enough times myself, so I knew this guy Nicky might show up in one day or one month.

After I had all my clothes and bathroom stuff unpacked, I started to get out a few personal items. A few paperback books, mostly about Indians, such as *Bury My Heart at Wounded Knee* and *Black Elk Speaks*. I got out these half a dozen posters I have, which are prints I ordered from an art museum. They are photographs of Indian art from caves and tipis.

The posters, which have a beige-colored background, are depictions of important tribal symbols and activities, such as the bear, the eagle, the raven, the elk, the buffalo hunt, and the capture of horses. The art is stick-figure art, because that is the Dakota tradition, especially when the pictures are used to tell a story.

I started putting the posters up with masking tape, being careful to get them mounted in a straight row.

"You must really like Indians," said Kinderhook.

"I don't just *like* Indians," I told him, "I have a connection with Indians."

"What do you mean, a connection?"

"Never mind. Forget it."

Then he said, "I'm pretty good at art. I could

draw you some better pictures than those stick fig-
ures if you want."

I couldn't believe it. "These posters are authentic."

"Sorry," he said.

By this time I'd had about all of Kinderhook I
could deal with. "Go to your room," I told him.
"Go somewhere. These are museum photographs of
real Indian art. The thing with actual art is, you
don't try to change it or make it suit you better."

"Well, excuuuuuuuuse me!" he said. He was
trying to imitate Steve Martin, the movie star; it was
real lame. He left without another word.

It was good to get rid of him, and not only because
he was irritating; I wanted to unpack my two most
valued possessions, my ceremonial pipe and my
journal. It wouldn't be easy to find a place for them,
because in group homes you never have any real
privacy. Your personal things are never secure the
way they should be, the way they would be in a
regular house.

Mr. Gibbs gave me the Sioux ceremonial a couple
of months after I moved in with him and Mrs.
Gibbs. He said he'd got it a long time ago on a
vacation out west, but he couldn't remember exactly
where. Of course my journal is where I keep my
notes and ideas; it's real personal and ultraprivate.

I finally put the ceremonial under some blue jeans
in the bottom drawer of the dresser. It seemed safe
enough for temporary, but I didn't know if it would
work for the long haul.

Before I decided where to put the journal, I spent

some time leafing through it. The journal wasn't cheap to buy; the pages are just blank, but it's a hardback book with a dark blue cover. Even though it cost quite a bit of money, I look at it as a wise investment. I've been moved around a lot, shuffled over from one placement to another, but the journal is something like a constant. No matter where I'm placed, it stays the same; it's still the same ideas and notes, and it's always me.

Anyway, I got to leafing through and rereading story notes I hadn't thought about for a while. There was one about this guy named Wintergreen, who is a very important executive in a huge corporation. The corporation is almost like an empire, they have important business deals with the U.S. government and also many foreign governments. Wintergreen has built up quite a few enemies, as anyone would in such a high position. One day, Wintergreen begins to develop this strange mental disease. The way it affects him is, he can't ignore anything, or put any information in the back of his mind. Everything he sees on the television news, everything stays right in the front of his mind at all times. His head is about ready to explode from this overload of data, so he has to move into this padded room without any windows, or radio, or TV, or any reading material. When his enemies find out about his condition, they conspire against him and rig this speaker into the ceiling of his padded room. Then they pipe this all-news radio station through the speaker until

Wintergreen can't stand it anymore, and he commits suicide.

After I finished reading through the Wintergreen notes, I came across another favorite story outline: This conspiracy of military officers has overthrown the U.S. government. The country is now under the control of these certain generals, who form a dictatorship. They use military police to enforce strict order in all parts of the country, which is a policy that makes most people happy. But after that, they go on this huge campaign for *efficiency*. One of the major aspects of this efficiency campaign is the elimination of everyone who is designated as a TUS. TUS is the abbreviation for people who *take up space*. People who take up space are people who don't make any contribution to the general welfare of the society. Like the ones who just feed their own face, watch a lot of TV, and go to bed. Or the people who sit around drinking beer and making a lot of public noise, like driving around aimlessly in a loud car or shooting off fireworks any time of year. This efficiency campaign has the population in a frenzy, as thousands of people suddenly realize that taking up space is about all they do. The new government has an agency that identifies everyone who is a TUS, and then the military police round them up and take them away for elimination.

I ended up reading these notes and outlines for quite a while. When I was finished, I put the journal in the one drawer in the nightstand next to the bed, where I could practically reach out and touch it.

There was no lock on the drawer, though, so I knew I'd probably end up taking it with me wherever I went.

My new social worker didn't come by until the next morning. She looked around fifty years old and she was big, maybe six feet or close to it. She wasn't fat, but she was what you might call bulky. Her name was Barb McGuire.

She said why don't we go out and get a donut, and I said okay. We took a ride in her car, which was an old station wagon with plenty of rust and rattles and a back window that didn't close all the way. While she was driving, she was eating from a bag of Fritos; she offered me some, but I said no thanks.

"Maybe we can visit a while," she said. "I'd like to get to know you a little bit if we're going to be working together. Then we can go to the high school and get you registered."

I didn't say anything.

"You'll be a little late. I hope you don't mind." She was still eating the Fritos. Her face was pock-marked with acne scars, and her voice was loud.

"It sounds okay to me," I said.

We stopped at a McDonald's restaurant. She got a briefcase from the backseat, then we went inside. We both had a cheese Danish and coffee. She asked me if I like coffee.

I told her if I didn't like it, I wouldn't be drinking it.

She laughed. "It'll stunt your growth."

"Let's say you're right," I said. "I'm trying to think of a reason to get any taller."

"Do they let you have coffee at Gates House?"

"I don't know. I don't know much about Gates House yet."

Then she lit up a cigarette and started telling me a few things about herself. "I'm brand new at this," she said. "Maybe you and I can help each other."

I asked her what she meant.

"I'm a late bloomer," she said. "I'm getting my degree in social work in another six weeks. A month after that, my high school class is having their thirtieth reunion. Most people get a college degree in four years, but I'm on the thirty-year plan, I guess." Then she started laughing again, real loud.

I guess I needed to say something. "Better late than never, huh?"

"That's how I look at it. Or try to. It just takes some of us a little longer to find ourselves. Anyway, I've only got four clients. I'll have a full caseload after I graduate. For right now, I'm afraid you're one of the guinea pigs."

This is just great, I thought to myself. I've got a social worker so green, she probably doesn't know the front door from the back. "What were you doing for the thirty years, before you went to college?" I asked.

"I was taking care of a husband and raising a son," she said. "I did some part-time secretarial work. I don't have much experience in the workplace, so I was serious when I said we'd have to help each other."

I could tell she was a person who meant well, but I could see how the system might eat her alive. As for helping her, I couldn't see how it was my job to baby-sit inexperienced social workers. All I really planned on doing was putting in my time until the legal age of eighteen, then finding my place in the Indian world.

She got some papers and folders out of her brief-case and started scrounging through them. Pretty soon after she put out the first cigarette, she lit up again.

"You know those cigarettes are bad for your health," I said.

"How well I know, please don't remind me. I'm trying to cut down, and someday I'll give them up completely." Then she put on a pair of glasses and said, "Do you remember your parents at all, Floyd?"

"No." This was going to be the same old questions.

"You never knew your father at all?"

"Not hardly. Maybe my mother didn't even know."

"You were living with your mother until you were four years old. But you don't remember a thing about her?"

"No. I remember a woman and a place. The place was a house with a porch and a big yard. I think there were cars in the yard, up on blocks. I know it was in Missouri, but that's just because I've been told it was; who knows one state from another when they're only four years old?"

"You've been living in a foster home?"

I nodded my head.

"A couple by the name of Gibbs, from down in Peoria."

"Mrs. Gibbs has diabetes," I said. "It's pretty serious. She was too sick to have foster kids anymore."

"Was that a good placement for you?" Barb asked.

"It was okay, I guess. It was better than a group home."

"Were you close to Mr. and Mrs. Gibbs?"

"I wouldn't say that. Mr. Gibbs wasn't a guy who did a lot of talking. He had a lot of mechanical talent, though; he had a real good workshop."

"Do you like to do mechanical work?"

"Yeah, I like it."

Barb was still shuffling papers. "You've lived in two other group homes and two other foster homes. You've crammed a lot of moving into your fifteen years, haven't you?"

I didn't say anything. People in social services have your files, so they read through your case history material and they think they know something about you. Like you could read the ingredients on a cereal box and you'd know what the cereal tastes like. If she really wanted to know something about me, she'd have to understand about my Indian destiny or get a look inside my journal. But I wasn't about to go into any of that.

Then she asked me what I thought about Gates House.

I just shrugged. "I haven't been there twenty-four hours yet. It's a group home, what can I say?"

"Do you like foster homes better than group homes?"

"It depends on the foster home."

She put out her cigarette and smiled at me. "You keep a tight lid on it, don't you, Floyd?"

She surprised me a little with that remark. "I don't know what you mean."

"You don't? What I mean is, you keep things inside."

I looked her in the eye. "Maybe that's true, I never thought about it. Is there something wrong with it?"

"It can't be good for you. Maybe you should loosen up."

"You get that way," I said.

"Maybe. Do you have to stay that way?"

I really didn't care for her approach at all. I hardly even knew her. I said, "What are we going to do, get psychological here?"

She was still smiling. "I guess we're not."

I wondered what the hell she meant by that remark. I didn't know what was happening here, but all I wanted was to get on with the next thing.

I guess she did, too. "Why don't we go on over to the high school," she said, "and get you registered?"

I told her thanks for the Danish and the coffee.

School registration was routine. Most of it was

handled by this guy named Mr. Saberhagen, who was an assistant principal but said he preferred to be called dean of students. He was a real crisp kind of a guy, buttoned down personally and when it came to his clothes. He spent a lot of time stretching his neck.

Since we were late, I didn't go to all my classes, but I went to some. I got a locker for P.E. People stared at me because I was new, but it didn't bother me; I've transferred to new schools enough times to be used to it.

My chemistry teacher was an old man named Mr. Mushrush. He had a hearing aid and seemed a little senile. He didn't have much control over the class. The students called him Mushy.

It was different in English class. The teacher, Mrs. Bluefish, was real edgy. She did a lot of pacing around and every once in a while she clapped her hands if she thought there was somebody with a wandering mind. But other times, she seemed to do the clapping just for emphasis. She had blue hair, which you sometimes see in ladies her age. Before class was over, she gave us an assignment to write a book report.

After supper, I signed myself out to take another walk, destination Vale Park. Kinderhook begged to come along, so I said okay.

There was a stream in the park with quite a few willow trees along the bank. There were scraps of willow bark on the ground, and some of them were pretty dry; I started picking them up and stuffing them into my pockets.

Kinderhook wanted to know why I was taking the willow bark.

"It's traditional in Sioux rituals and on solemn occasions. They smoke it in their ceremonial pipes."

"Is it like a drug or something?"

"It's got nothing to do with drugs. It's just a tradition."

"How come you always talk about the Sioux?" he wanted to know.

"The real name is Dakota," I told him. "That's the Indian name. Sioux is a French word, and if you want the truth, it's not really authentic."

"Okay, but that's not what I asked."

Kinderhook was such a pest. I said to him, "I had a vision last summer. I believe I was a Dakota in a past life. It's my destiny to become an Indian."

Maybe it was more than he wanted to deal with; anyway, it shut him up.

On the way back to Gates House, he said he wanted to watch *The Wizard*.

"So watch it," I said. "There's a TV in the lounge."

"Slive will never let me," said Kinderhook. "He doesn't really care about watching anything else, he just likes to take it out on me."

I knew who Slive was; his room was at the other end of the hall. I could tell just by looking at him that he was your basic intimidator. I felt a little sorry for Kinderhook, so I said, "Maybe he won't be there.

Maybe you can watch what you want."

"He'll be there. He's always there."

If Kinderhook wanted me to get involved in his TV hassles, he could kiss that off. If you felt too sorry for a guy like him, you could get sucked in.

When I got back to my room, I spent some time brainstorming out a few notes on the Stone Boy legend, trying to see if I might be able to work it into the English class book report.

After that I went down to the lounge to check out the ten o'clock news. There was no one there, so I switched on channel nine. I was only there about two minutes when Mrs. Grice came in. She had her teeth out and was wearing a faded old housecoat. She parked herself on the couch without saying a word.

She had a big cellophane bag of cheese popcorn. She was trying to eat the popcorn without any teeth. Between the way she smacked her lips all the time, and crackled the cellophane bag, I just couldn't stand it. I liked to watch the news, but not at this price.

I left the lounge and went to bed.

CHAPTER FOUR

Looking back, it seems like it started getting off the track that Sunday morning we went to church. It was a big Baptist church. There were about eight of us there, along with a house staff member named Marty. His title was a specialist; one thing you learn about the system is, everybody who works for it gets a heavy-duty title.

The policy at Gates House was you had to go to church at least two Sundays out of the month. Because of all my background in social services, going to church was nothing new to me. I've done quite a bit of reading of religious material, and I would say I have a decent amount of Bible knowledge. Of course my highest interest is in Dakota religion, although I have spent quite a bit of time reading about Pawnee beliefs, as the Pawnee gave a lot of extra attention to the supernatural.

Anyway, on this Sunday morning, the minister, whose name was Reverend Braithwaite, was preaching a sermon on miracles in the Bible. I was pretty interested because the things he was talking about were a lot like certain miraculous stories in Indian religion.

After church, there was the customary socializing out on the steps. For some reason, the reverend seemed to take a lot of interest in those of us from Gates House.

He wanted to know my name, so Marty introduced us. Then he asked me what I thought of his sermon on miracles.

"It reminded me a lot of Indian miracles I've read about," I told him.

"What's that?"

If he was interested, I was more than happy to tell him.

First, I told him the story of Bull-all-the-time, who was a Crow chief. He was hunting alone one day, when he broke his ankle, and had to rest on this huge rock. All of a sudden he was face-to-face with a rattlesnake, which was coiled and ready to strike. Using total concentration, Chief Bull-all-the-time stared into the eyes of the snake until he hypnotized it and it just fell over.

Well, Reverend Braithwaite did not appreciate this story at all, which came as a surprise to me. In fact, he got uptight. He said, "That's an amusing story, but I can assure you it has nothing to do with the miraculous powers of the apostles in the New Testament." He went on to say that the apostles used the direct power of Almighty God to heal the blind and the lame.

At this point I thought it might make him feel

better if I talked about some healing, so I told him about this Indian shaman who built a fire and coaxed evil spirits out of sick people and into the fire.

"A shaman is simply a medicine man, young man," he said to me.

"That's true," I said.

"I can assure you these superstitious, heathen stories have nothing to do with the revealed truth found in God's Word." He seemed good and pissed.

By this time everyone was getting tense, including me and including the other people who were standing around, as it was obvious that Reverend Braithwaite was highly worked up. All I had wanted to do was swap a few stories, but I could see that it wasn't going to work, so I made the suggestion that we should just drop the subject. Unfortunately, he wasn't ready to drop the subject.

He looked at Marty and then back at me. He said, "Does this young man have even basic Christian understanding?" He asked me, "Do you understand that in the person of Jesus Christ, God Almighty Himself has come to dwell among us?"

I really didn't know what to say, not with the reverend in his worked-up condition. I didn't want to lie. I looked back and forth between Marty and Reverend Braithwaite, hoping Marty might say it was time to leave, but he looked like he had a little confusion of his own.

I thought maybe I could mellow things out by being polite, so I told Reverend Braithwaite I thought Jesus Christ was very wise. Instead of helping the situation, this just about flipped him out.

"Wise?? Did you say wise?" Reverend Braithwaite had a look on his face like I'd just told him Russia was the best country to live in. "Wise is a word for ordinary mortals. Wisdom is not something the Son of God has need of!"

By this time he was beginning to sputter, with a little bit of drool trickling on his chin. I can't remember all of what he said, but things just went from bad to worse. He even got on Marty's case and told him there needed to be better religious training at Gates House.

Somehow, Marty finally got us excused, and we were in the van heading home. I told him I was sorry for what happened, that I hadn't planned any trouble. He kept his eyes on his driving. He was a guy who tended not to talk much. He said, "People get ultraserious when it comes to their religion; they tend to lose their sense of humor. What can I say?"

Unfortunately, Mrs. Grice wasn't quite that calm when she heard about it. Not that you'd expect her to be. She was all over my case; she told me the incident would reflect bad on Gates House.

"We've had a relationship with First Baptist for years," she said. "Reverend Braithwaite has even taught confirmation classes for our residents, on his own time."

I told her I was sorry, but I didn't do anything wrong.

She said it looked like I needed religious training,

so she'd try and get me signed up for Bible study or confirmation class.

I looked right at her. "You've got to be kidding," I said.

"Don't you use a tone with me," she said. "I'm not going to warn you again."

I was starting to get pissed. "All I did was tell him a couple of stories about Indian religion."

"Indian stories?"

"I happen to know a thing or two about Indian religion. I thought he might be interested. He asked me, right?"

"Let me tell you something. Your job is not to tell him anything. When you go to church, your job is to listen."

I felt myself getting more pissed, but I figured what the hell, what good would it do?

Suppertime started out okay, but then it went downhill quick. Kinderhook got caught putting dinner rolls in his pockets. Mrs. Grice called it stealing food, but how it could be stealing when it was food put on the table for us to eat, I'm not sure.

Anyway, she went charging over to the bulletin board, where she got herself a piece of chalk. Then she used the chalk to mark a big X on the floor, right where the kitchen goes into the lounge. She made Kinderhook stand on the X. He was a little slow getting in gear, so she got him by the ear and hustled his ass over to the spot. He was bigger than she was; it looked like Mrs. Grice was hauling this pile of dough. It would have been funny, except you had to feel sorry for him.

He had to stand on the X while we ate the rest of our supper, which was most of it. He turned his back and faced the lounge, out of embarrassment. His red neck was the only part of him that wasn't white.

It was my night for kitchen crew, so after supper I was doing cleanup with this guy named Rabe. We could have finished up by six-thirty easily, but with Mrs. Grice, you learned right away not to do your chores too fast. If you finished quick, she just gave you more.

She showed up about seven o'clock and wanted to know why we weren't done yet. I was sponging out the stove burners; I told her we were going for excellence. It went over her head. She took a glance at Kinderhook on the X, then went back to her room without saying anything.

Slive was watching TV in the lounge. After Mrs. Grice disappeared, he went by and gave Kinderhook a goose. That was when Kinderhook started crying; there wasn't any sound, but you could see his shoulders shaking up and down.

We were done with the cleanup, so I went up to my room. There was a fire alarm by the exit door; I thought about pulling it so the whole house would have to evacuate. That would get Kinderhook off the X, and maybe it would slip Mrs. Grice's mind afterward. But I figured I was already in enough trouble for one day.

By the time I went back down, it was eight o'clock. Kinderhook was still there. That was two hours on the X. He kept shifting his weight from one leg to the other, but there was nothing to lean on.

Some guys were watching TV in the lounge, so I sat down on one of the chairs; I didn't pay too much attention to what program was on.

That was when Marty came in, carrying groceries. He set his bags on the counter and started putting things away in the cupboards and the refrigerator. He took a look at Kinderhook and then he looked at me. For a fraction of a second our eyes met. Then he went back to work putting more groceries away.

It was a real moment. He knew and I knew. It wasn't right to put Kinderhook through this, not over a couple of rolls. Marty knew what a hairbag Mrs. Grice was, but he was just an underling, he wasn't about to cross her. That's the system in a nutshell. You're just a cog that the system needs, or it chews you up and spits you out. There's no place to be who you are, that part gets worn away.

It was three in the morning when I woke up because of some noise out in the street. It was only a car with a loud muffler, but since I was awake, I got up and snuck down to the kitchen. I was barefoot and didn't make a sound; the only light was a small fluorescent tube over the sink. It was a decent enough light once my eyes got used to it.

There was a moist sponge in a number-ten can

under the sink. I took it over and scrubbed the X off the floor. I scrubbed until there was no sign of it left; I'm not sure why.

Then I went back to bed.

It was a couple days after that when Mrs. Bluefish sent me down to the office of Mr. Saberhagen, the assistant principal. I had no idea what it was all about, but I knew it couldn't be good. I sat in the office to wait, while these two secretaries answered the phone and did a lot of file work.

One of them finally told me I could see Mr. Saberhagen now. I went in and he said, "Please have a seat, Floyd," so I sat down next to his desk.

Mr. Saberhagen is a stern, formal guy. I doubt if he ever cracks a joke about anything. He is bald back to the crown of his head, but he lets the back part of his hair grow real long and then combs it all forward. He uses hair spray or something to hold it in place.

"This shouldn't take too long, Floyd. I just need to have a little chat with you about your footwear."

I looked down. I was wearing my Dakota moccasins, which come up to about midcalf.

"What do you call those, Floyd?"

"What do I call them? I call them by their name. Moccasins."

"I'd watch that tone of voice if I were you, Floyd." He cleared his throat, stretched his neck like he usually does, and went on: "Mrs. Bluefish feels that your moccasins are not appropriate dress for school.

I'm afraid I have to agree with her."

I couldn't believe it. This whole thing was going to be about my *moccasins*, as if there was something wrong with them.

I said, "They're appropriate for me."

"They're not appropriate for *school*, Floyd. They may be appropriate for certain social events, or for casual wear around the home, but not for school."

I was beginning to get a little pissed. I said to him, "My moccasins are authentic, handmade by the Dakota. They cost me fifty bucks. I had to get them mail order from a trading post in Wisconsin. These are not discount store merchandise."

"The value of your moccasins is not the issue here; you're missing the point. We do have a school dress code, which is spelled out in the student handbook. Have you read your copy?"

I didn't say anything. The *student handbook*, whatever that was, was probably buried back in my room, along with all the other handouts and printed stuff I got on my first day of school.

Saberhagen went on. "Part of my job is to educate students in the social arts. Let me show you a few items here that might help you understand."

As soon as he said this, he got out several catalogues and put them on the desk. It turned out they were manuals on proper dress, dressing to fit the occasion, finding the right combinations, and so on. He showed me several pages on shoes; he showed me a large picture of these black wing tips, and he asked me, now wouldn't I really like to have a pair like that?

I couldn't believe it. Wing-tip shoes weigh about six pounds each, with a leather sole about as thick as a dictionary, and the toe is all covered with these leather whirls that have little holes punched in them. Lawyers wear them when they go to court; somebody else may wear them, too, I'm not sure. But it would be hard to imagine anything more out of touch with the Indian way.

"Well, what do you say?" Saberhagen wanted to know.

"What I say is, my moccasins aren't hurting anybody."

"I've warned you once about your tone of voice, and I'm not going to do so again. I'm asking you what you intend to do about your footwear."

I got good and pissed, which is unusual for me. I can usually slough off these more or less insulting situations without any trouble. I probably should have let the whole thing drop, but I said, "I wouldn't wear wing-tip shoes even if I got them for free. As long as it doesn't rain, I'm going to keep on wearing my moccasins."

Mr. Saberhagen slammed his catalogues shut. "That's it," he said, and he stood up. "If you think you can speak to me in this manner, in my office, then you've got another think coming. Your first detention begins immediately, and you will serve detentions every day until the end of the week."

Then he wrote out the detentions and handed

them to me. He had a look on his face like he expected me to say something.

"Is that all?" I asked.

"Yes. That is all."

After my last class, I went down to the auditorium, which is also the study hall, to serve the detention. I was a little bummed out to be doing time with all these troublemakers. I freely admit to being a little weird, but I have never in my life been a troublemaker. Troublemakers commit deliberate acts to cause other people grief.

I gave the detention slip to Mr. Porter, one of the coaches, who told me to sit in 16B. Our school is real old, and the study hall desks are these double desks, with only a thin wooden armrest between one person and the next.

It turned out that 16B was right next to a sleazeball named Nicky in 16A. I couldn't remember seeing him around, but he seemed so enthusiastic about having some company that he told me his name right off.

"What are you in for?" he asked. Saying this, he took out a switchblade with about a five-inch blade, and started using it to clean his fingernails. His nails were long, with a lot of built-up dirt. He wasn't getting them too clean, but he did dig out these little wads of dirt on the tip of his knife blade and scraped them off on the armrest. Then he started picking his *nose* with the switchblade. I said to to myself, *Is this a troublemaker or what? What am I doing here?*

"Hey, man, what are you in for?" he asked again.

I showed him my moccasins. "Saberhagen doesn't like my moccasins."

"What's wrong with them?"

"He says they're not appropriate for school."

"I'd say it's none of his business."

"That's what I told him," I said.

"Way to go. It's good to take no shit offa him."

"If it's so good, why am I here?"

I guess that gave him something to think about because he stopped talking. It didn't help the way he smelled, though. He smelled like he must wash about once a month. We've got a lot of guys like him in school; they should round them up every couple of days and take them down to the locker room and scour them down in the shower. I would recommend S.O.S. pads and Comet cleanser. I'm not sure what you could do with their clothes. I guess they'd have to have different ones.

I looked around the study hall; there were maybe thirty people serving detentions, which left about three hundred empty seats. It seemed like a joke that I had to sit this close to a guy who smelled bad and was a pest besides. I thought about asking Mr. Porter to assign me a different seat, but I didn't know if you had any rights when you were serving detention.

I put it out of my mind. I shifted to the left as far as I could and took out the handout Mrs. Bluefish had given us in English class. It was information about a story-writing contest. I started reading through the guidelines. You could submit a story if

72

you were under seventeen, and the deadline was the end of May. It told how long the story was supposed to be, how you had to type it double-spaced, and so forth. The person who won the contest would have their story published in some magazine I'd never heard of called *Script*, and would receive a cash prize of a thousand dollars. I consider myself a writer, so I found that I had a pretty bona fide interest in this contest.

"What's that?" It was him again.

"It's nothing."

"But what *is* it?" Nicky insisted.

So I showed the contest form to him. Not that I thought he'd have any real interest.

He didn't. "Want to know what I'm in for?" he said.

"Not particularly."

"You gotta hear this. You know Mushy?"

He was talking about the chemistry teacher. "I know him," I said.

"Well, I brought this dog whistle to class. The sound is so high, a human ear can't hear it. But when I blew it in class, it like blew all his circuits. It was choice." Telling this, Nicky had an ear-to-ear grin plastered on his face.

"That is clever," I said. Mr. Mushrush wears this old-fashioned type of hearing aid, the kind that has a battery pack that you keep in a shirt pocket. There're some guys in my chemistry class who make a high-pitched hum, with their mouths closed. Mr. Mushrush thinks it's some kind of electronic feedback, so he usually starts slapping at the battery pack. I have to admit it was kind of funny, in a juvenile sort of way, the first time I watched it.

Nicky had more to tell me. "Last time I was in for setting off cherry bombs in the girls' bathroom," he said. "But this dog whistle was really choice. I wish you could've been there." He still had the grin frozen on his face. He told about these things with the kind of pride you'd expect from somebody who'd just won a college scholarship.

When the bell rang, I asked Mr. Porter if I could have a different seat for my other detentions.

"You'll keep the seat I gave you," he said.

Thanks to a phone call from the school, Mrs. Grice knew about the detentions by the time I got back to Gates House. After she chewed my ass for being rebellious and disrespectful, she informed me I was now on probation.

I told her I didn't do anything wrong, but all she said was, "I don't want to hear it."

Then she spelled out the terms of my probation. It was more or less like being grounded. I couldn't go on any special activities, unless they were required by the agency; I wouldn't have any sign-out privileges to go places on my own. I was required to take a chart to school every day and get it signed by Mr. Saberhagen to show that my behavior was appropriate.

That was about it. The last thing she told me was, "Naturally, I'll be calling your social worker." She was popping her loose lip a mile a minute.

"Naturally," I said.

"I sincerely hope that's not a tone of voice."

"I'm just trying to be agreeable here."

Then she told me I needed to go to my room, which was where I wanted to go anyway.

Barb came over after supper. She asked me what I was working on, so I showed her the form for the story contest. She sort of skimmed it, then said, "Do you like to write?"

"I like to think of myself as a writer," I said. I pointed to my journal, which was out on the table. "I keep a record of story notes and ideas," I said.

It seemed to impress her. "I tried to write some poems once, when my son was real small. I guess they were okay, in a greeting card sort of way."

I didn't know what I was supposed to say about it, but then it was kind of funny; not humorous, but strange: She was handing me back the contest form and I saw her wiping a tear from her eye. Like something just surged up in her emotions and then disappeared. I didn't know what to make of it, but it made me a little edgy.

She asked me if I was going to enter the contest.

"I was thinking about it," I said.

"Go for it. Maybe you'll write the story that wins first prize." Then she made a quick shift. "We need to talk. You can't smoke in here, so how 'bout if we go outside and sit on the stoop?"

It didn't matter to me. As soon as we got to the stoop, she lit up. "You've got yourself in detention and on probation. Why don't you tell me what happened?"

"We had a shoe controversy," I said. I gave her a basic summary of my meeting with Saberhagen.

Barb looked at my moccasins and said, "What's the problem with them?"

"Saberhagen says they're not appropriate for school."

"They look presentable to me, and they look like good quality."

"They are good quality. These are authentic Dakota moccasins, handmade."

She looked a little impatient. I noticed she was wearing blue jeans and a sweat shirt, not that it mattered to me. Her clothes were her business. She said, "So what's the problem?"

"I got pissed and gave him some lip. That's the real reason I got the detentions, if you want the truth. I told him my moccasins weren't hurting anybody, and I was going to go right on wearing them."

"All right, it was a mistake to lip off. You can see that as well as I can. But I'll go in and talk to him; there has to be a way to sort this out."

She doesn't have a clue, I thought to myself. She thinks she can walk into Saberhagen's office and use logic on him. She probably even thinks she could use logic on Mrs. Grice.

There must have been a look on my face, because Barb said, "You don't want me to talk to him."

I shrugged. "You can do anything you want, but

it's a waste of time. Saberhagen says my moccasins are against the school dress code."

She wanted to know where she could read the school dress code, so I told her it was supposedly in the student handbook.

"If you don't mind, I'd like to borrow your copy," she said.

"I don't mind. You want it now?"

"Not right now, just get it for me before I leave. While we're at it here, would you mind telling me what happened Sunday morning?"

"Sunday morning?"

"At church."

"Oh, that." I laughed. "That's a joke, that was nothing."

"Mrs. Grice didn't think it was nothing. She was upset about it."

This was getting on my nerves. "That's Mrs. Grice's favorite game. Making something out of nothing."

"Floyd, please just tell me what happened. I'd like to hear your side of it." I could see Mrs. Grice looking at us from her window. I had this thought, that besides her usual disapproval of me, she was probably disapproving of Barb's smoking.

Anyway, I summed up the give-and-take between me and the Reverend Braithwaite. For a conclusion I said, "I really didn't mean to cause him any grief, but he asked. All I really wanted to do was swap a few stories about miracles. But he came unglued, and once he got his teeth in it, he wouldn't let go."

"You really love Indians, don't you?" Barb said.

I had to think a minute. "I'd have to say I feel connected to the Dakota; I believe my destiny is locked in with them. Whether or not love has anything to do with it, I couldn't say."

"When you say destiny, what do you mean?"

She seemed sincerely interested, so I said, "I believe that you come back in another life many times. In some of these lives, you get off the track, which means you are separated from your true destiny. When you're off the track, if you don't reflect on the inner person that you are, you will spend your life uptight and out of touch."

"You mean like reincarnation," she said. "I've got a hamster at home. Do you think he was once Henry the Eighth or Joan of Arc?"

She said it in a certain way that I could tell she wasn't being smart-ass. "No, you don't come back as a dog or a cat; all your lives are human lives. I wrote a story about it once."

"Why don't you give me a summary of the story?"

It was unusual for somebody to ask me this type of question, but she still seemed sincere about it, so I said, "There was this guy named Galsworthy. His destiny was to be a plumber, and he should have known it, because he liked to fool around with fixtures in his house, especially leaky faucets and running toilets. But he ignored all the signs; all he wanted was to be a rich and powerful executive. He ended up hooked on cocaine and booze, and jumping out of a tall building."

She had a smile on her face. "Maybe you could use that story for your contest."

I shrugged. "It's a possibility. I've got lots of outlines. Anyway, you can spend lots of your lives in misery if you never get in touch with your destiny."

"Does this come from Indian research?"

"Not really. Indian religion is not big into past and future lives. It's basically my own view."

She was laughing. "No offense, Floyd, but it does sound a little weird."

"Let's put it this way. It's weird enough that I'm on probation."

"Come on, lighten up. That's not what I mean."

I knew she wasn't putting me down, but I was trying to make a point. "It's weird or not weird, depending on how you look at it. One thing I've noticed about beliefs is, if a lot of people believe in a thing, it's not considered weird, but if only a few people believe in it, it's off-the-wall. You can believe everything written in the Bible, even a part like God coming down out of the sky to have a wrestling match with Abraham, and nobody questions it."

"I understand what you're getting at," she said. "In lots of other cultures, your belief about looking for a destiny in a series of lives would be considered normal."

"I'm not pissed at you, I'm just trying to make a point."

She nodded her head. "I also understand that you didn't mean any harm when you spoke to Reverend Braithwaite. I'll talk to Mrs. Grice about it."

She was still into that. "If you want to," I said.

"You don't want me to."

"It's not that," I said. In a way though, it was; I've learned you can't depend on other people to fight your battles for you. You have to depend on yourself, because that's all there is. I didn't want to go into that, though. I just said to her, "I've been through this kind of crap before. My advice to you is, don't waste your time."

"Since it's my time, how about if I decide how to waste it?"

All I could do was shrug again. "Whatever."

She was looking at her watch. "It's almost eight-thirty, I need to be going. Would you please get me that student handbook?"

I got her the handbook.

CHAPTER FIVE

For a week or ten days, things were cool. I was sneaking out the fire escape every once in a while, mostly to chill out in Vale Park, or sometimes to go to the library to look at materials for my English class book report. Mrs. Grice never caught me, though, and nobody turned me in.

But then I came home from school one day and made a discovery that really funked me.

My new roommate, the guy named Nicky, turned out to be the same hairball that sat next to me when I was serving detentions. I couldn't believe it; I remembered that Kinderhook had told me the name was Nicky, but who would've put two and two together?

When I got there, he was in the middle of unpacking his stuff and putting up *Iron Maiden* and *Harley-Davidson* posters on his half of the walls. He had this big grin as soon as he saw me. "Yo, bro. We meet again."

I didn't say anything. I sat down on my bed and

wondered, *Why me?* I started putting my books away.

While he was unpacking, he was telling me how he'd been hung out for about six weeks, hoping they'd let him stay with his mother, but now it looked like this placement at Gates was more or less permanent. I didn't say much; not that I get any pleasure from another person being hung out, but I didn't want to give him too much encouragement.

When I was serving detentions, I made a point of trying to ignore him, but now I was checking him out. Not being too obvious about it, of course. He was about five feet two and weighed maybe one hundred pounds at the most. Like a lot of the punks you run into, he wanted to look like a tough guy. His hair was long and greased back like Fonzie on *Happy Days*. He had on this black leather motorcycle jacket, even though it was the month of May and real warm, and engineer boots with metal heel taps. He had a big Harley-Davidson belt buckle that said, *Ride to Live, Live to Ride*.

I got out my journal and propped myself up on the bed. Trying to ignore him, I started jotting down what would be the qualities of the ideal roommate. He would be clean. He would be neat and keep all his stuff on his own half. He would be quiet and mind his own business. I began to realize I was describing myself.

Nicky kept trying to interest me in the stuff he was unpacking. He started opening up *Iron Horse* magazines, and showing me pictures of naked girls sitting on big Harley hogs.

"Check it out," he said, with the big grin. "Is she prime or what?"

I thought about telling him he might go on pro if Mrs. Grice found the magazines, but then I figured, what the hell, he was big enough to sink or swim on his own.

Then he saw my ceremonial on the dresser and wanted to know about it.

"It's a Dakota ceremonial pipe," I said. "It's authentic."

"What, do you smoke it?"

"I don't smoke it the way a person smokes a pipe, you know, to *smoke*. No one does. It's like a religious item; it's used by the Indians for special occasions."

Then he wanted to know what it was made of. Not that I thought he had any real interest in Dakota culture, but it would be easier to answer his question than to find a way to put him off.

"The whole pipe is made of catlinite," I told him.

"What the hell is that?"

"It's a kind of red stone that gets mined in places like Minnesota and the Dakotas. That's why the pipe is authentic. If you buy a so-called Indian pipe in a mall or someplace, it will be made of wood or plastic."

"What are the feathers for?"

"I'm getting to that. The small ones represent the four corners of the universe. The black one is for the west, the white one is for the north, the red one is for the east, and the yellow one is for the south. The eagle feather is the most important one; it represents the Great Spirit, *Wakan Tanka*."

He said, "You're really into Indians, man." But I could tell he was already bored. I put the pipe away, under some clothes in the bottom dresser drawer. It wasn't supposed to be out in view anyway.

Then he wanted to know about my journal and what I was writing in it. I wasn't anxious to go into a lot of detail, so I just sort of rifled the pages to show the scope of it. I told him some of it was diary stuff, but a lot of it was story notes and outlines.

"You wrote all those stories?"

"Like I said, these are mostly outlines and notes. Sometimes I get one finished." I hoped that would be the end of the conversation.

Unfortunately, he remembered that story contest form from the first day we were in detention together. He pestered me a dozen times to tell him about one of the stories, one that I might use in the contest.

To get him off my back, I finally said, "Just one, and then we drop it. I'm not in the head for this."

It seemed to satisfy him, so I found the one about the military takeover where the agents round up everyone who is a TUS and take them away for elimination. I didn't actually *read* the story to him, I basically just skimmed my notes and summed up.

"What's a TUS?" Nicky wanted to know.

"Weren't you listening? TUS is an acronym for

anyone who just takes up space. People who make no contribution."

He said, "How are they eliminated?"

"It doesn't really make any difference," I said.

"But I mean how? Do they get the chair or the gas chamber? Maybe it's up against the wall in front of the firing squad. How are they eliminated?"

I tried to explain. "It doesn't really matter. The point is, if all you do is take up space, you are targeted for elimination."

Then he asked me: "Is this for real?"

I almost fell over from disbelief. "Don't you get it? This is an outline for a *story*."

"Yeah, but if this was for real, I'd like to be one of the military police who goes around and croaks these losers."

What could you say to such a person? I didn't have the heart to tell him that if this was for real, he would probably be a TUS with a very limited future.

A few days after that, Barb came over in her car. She said she had a couple of things to discuss, but Gates House was not the best place to talk, so maybe we should take a ride.

We stopped at a Dairy Queen to get a small cone, which we ate in the car. She was pretty good at eating and driving at the same time. We talked about Indians for a while; I don't remember the conversation in particular, but she seemed to have more than your average interest in Plains Indian customs.

"I'm graduating next week," she told me. "I'll be an honest-to-god MSW."

"That's good," I said. "Congratulations."

She was talking with a mouthful: "I'll be getting a full caseload. That means less time to spend with you."

Actually, it was a relief to hear it. Not that I didn't like her — her redeeming features were fairly obvious. I wondered where we were going and what it was we were supposed to be doing.

We ended up at her house, which was a big old two-story with lots of shade trees. She walked me through the backyard, which was big, and in through the back door. I guess it was because of the shade trees, but the rooms in the house seemed kind of dark.

The furniture in her living room had a lot of mileage on it, but it was homey. There was a military sword above the fireplace mantel. Barb said it belonged to her husband. There were two large framed pictures on the mantel, one of her husband and one of her son. The son was in an army uniform.

"He died two years ago in Lebanon," she told me. "There were seven GIs killed in a terrorist bombing at a railroad station."

It was sad, because I knew her husband was dead, too. "I'm sorry," I mumbled. It was all I could think to say.

"So am I," she said. Then she turned and headed for the kitchen. I could tell she was wiping tears, even though I couldn't see her face. Then I got a little pissed. She was supposed to be my *social worker*, for christ sake. What were we doing at her house looking at meaningful pictures and stopping on the way for ice-cream cones?

Eventually, I followed her into the kitchen. She gave me a Pepsi and offered me some popcorn, but I said no thanks; all I could think of was no-teeth Mrs. Grice and her crackling cellophane bags.

Barb said to me, "I got your probation lifted."

"Oh, yeah?"

"We had a meeting. Mrs. Grice was there. Also Mr. Wagner, the head of the agency, and the agency psychologist."

"Sounds just like a staffing."

"Not quite on the scale of a staffing. I got all the facts and I told them I couldn't see how you deserved to be on probation. I don't think I made myself very popular, especially with Mrs. Grice."

I suppose she thought I should be gushing all over with gratitude or something, when my probation was over in two weeks anyway.

"You're not happy," she said. "I thought it would make you happy to be off probation."

What did she want me to say? Why couldn't I have an old worn-out social worker who just went through the motions? I said, "What I want with Mrs. Grice is to turn invisible. She already watches me like a hawk, only now it'll be even more so."

"A good point," said Barb. "Which leads me to a question: Is this a good placement for you?"

"I don't know what that means. You get placed

and then you get placed again. Some of them are better than others."

"What it means is, are you happy with your placement?"

"Happy?" She was getting me pissed and doubly pissed that I was letting myself get dragged into this conversation. "You get the shitheads like Mrs. Grice and you do whatever it takes. Sometimes you get better placements and life gets easier."

"I have a better idea. Why not try for the best possible placement, especially if you're in an unhappy situation?"

"You think that's a better idea?"

"I guess I must, or I wouldn't have said it."

She just didn't get it. She was too green to get it. She needed to get the shit kicked out of her a couple of times and then maybe she'd understand. Only I didn't care to be the guinea pig for her to learn on. I changed my approach: "I don't want to talk about a new placement. I don't want to get hung out again."

"Please tell me more."

"Why?"

She shrugged. "Maybe I'll learn something." She lit up one of her Marlboro Lights.

"The thing that's worse than getting a bad placement is the way they leave you hanging when they know they're going to find a new placement for you, but they don't know where they're going to put you, or how soon."

"You're talking about the uncertainty," she said. "You're neither fish nor fowl."

"Right. They start having staffings on you, and they decide you do need a new placement. So you just sort of hang there, maybe a month, maybe three months, maybe even longer, and you don't feel like you belong where you are, but there's no other place for you to go."

She was looking at me. I didn't want that, either. She said to me, "I understand what you're telling me."

"If this is sympathy, I don't want it," I said. "I don't want sympathy and I don't want pity. I also don't want you fighting my battles for me."

"You know what I think, Floyd? You turn everything in."

"I turn everything in?"

"You can't turn everything in on yourself. Some things you have to turn out and ask for help."

"You get that way," I said. I couldn't remember the last time I'd had a conversation like this. Maybe never.

She went on. "It never crossed your mind to ask for help when you went on probation. I don't think it crossed your mind that you even have rights."

"I'm not a whiner."

"It's not whining to ask for help."

"I'll tell you this much about my destiny."

"You want to talk about your Indian destiny? Are we changing the subject?"

"Maybe yes, and maybe no. Here's my point:

There's an inside home and an outside home. Your inside home is the things you believe in, such as your goals. In my case it's wrapped up in my destiny. Your outside home is your placement. If you're together on the inside home, you've more or less gotten yourself outside the power of the system. It doesn't matter a hell of a lot what they do with your outside home."

Barb was putting out her cigarette. "You do have interesting thoughts," she said. "But I would need some time to ponder that. Let's table the talk about a new placement. We won't bring it up again unless you say so."

I wanted to tell her that'll be the day, but I just said okay.

Then she said, "You're probably wondering why I brought you over here."

"I'm wondering what?"

"Why I brought you to my home. There has to be a reason, right?"

I told her it must be the conversation we just had.

She waved her hand. "Not even close. Follow me." She went out the back door, heading for the garage. A little confused, I followed along.

The garage was big, with lots of tools hung on pegboard; it had that smell I really like, the smell of old oil and dirt mixed together.

Barb said, "My husband was a handyman. A real do-it-yourselfer." But you could tell that wasn't what was really on her mind. She was rummaging through this big wooden cabinet.

She brought out an old, brown baseball with a couple of loose stitches, and two baseball mitts. One was an ancient catcher's mitt, and the other was a more modern fielder's glove.

"Baseball," she said.

"Mhmm."

"How would you like to be on a baseball team?"

Naturally, I didn't have an answer ready for this.

"They're starting up a PONY league this summer. They'll have actual big league uniforms. How would you like to play for the Cubs?"

"A baseball team?" I said.

"I have a good friend named Nolan," she said. "He farms west of town. He's going to coach the team. If you want to play, all you have to do is say the word."

"This is why you brought me to your house?"

"I think you need to be involved in more activities with other kids. I thought maybe a baseball team would be just the thing."

"When does this league start?" I asked.

"The second week of June. What do you say? You ever play the game?" I wondered why she was putting on the baseball cap.

I shrugged. "I'm not a jock or anything, but I've played a little baseball in my time. This will be wholesome, right? This will be good for me."

"Don't be negative. I can vouch for Nolan, and I think you might enjoy it."

"I'm not being negative. I'll think about it."

"Good. That's the spirit. Here, put this on and

we'll see what you've got." She was handing me the fielder's glove.

"We're going to play baseball? Now?"

"And why not? Didn't I put my own son through six years of organized baseball?"

The next thing I knew, Barb and I were about fifty feet apart in her backyard, with her in front of a toolshed and me beside a birdbath. She was telling me to "burn 'em in," as she put it.

I threw her a few, but I almost started laughing, it was so wholesale comical. She had the baseball cap on backward, the way catchers do, and her catcher's mitt, which looked like a model from about 1900, had about as much shape as a throw pillow. It didn't have any pocket in it at all.

That wasn't even half as funny as this steady stream of lingo coming out of her mouth: "Whatta ya say, you 'n' me, babe, rock 'n' fire, whatta ya say." I burned 'em in for maybe fifteen or twenty minutes. I don't think she caught a single pitch I threw; every ball bounced off her pillow mitt the way it would if you threw it against a mattress.

At least none of the pitches hit her in the head, and I had to give her one thing: She was a good sport. When we were done, she said I had potential.

One day not too long after that, Mrs. Bluefish asked me to stay after class. I knew she had to okay your outline before you could go ahead and write your actual book report, so I figured it had something to do with that.

My report was on the Stone Boy legend. The Stone Boy legend, which is one of the most important Dakota myths, goes basically like this: A young woman was living with her brothers, who kept going out to hunt, but not returning. Before long, the young woman found herself living alone.

One day when the young woman was fetching water, she accidently swallowed a pebble, which made her pregnant. Of course this was a miracle. She gave birth at last to a boy whose flesh was made of stone. She knew he was destined to be a great hero, but she didn't know how or when.

When Stone Boy became a young man, he went on a long hunting trip. He came to this grim valley ruled by *Iya*, the Evil One. Stone Boy realized that *Iya* was holding his uncles and ancestors captive in semideath.

To free his ancestors, he had to escape a shower of boulders that *Iya* poured on him, and he had to fight the thundering herds of the Buffalo People that *Iya* sent. The Evil One even took the form of a gigantic tree, whose limbs were all serpents. Stone Boy used a shield and spear to hack away on the serpents, but there were too many, and they kept regenerating.

Each time he fought with the serpent tree, he ended up limping back to the tipi of Old Woman, who nursed his wounds and tried to advise him.

Anyway, Mrs. Bluefish was looking over my outline. She asked, "Did the Stone Boy figure free his ancestors?"

"He freed them all," I told her. "That was his heroic mission."

"How did he accomplish it?"

"That's the part I'm not sure about. The legend is told in different ways, and some of the tellings aren't complete. That's what I wanted to do in the book report — sort of combine the different versions and see if I can come up with a common denominator."

"That's what I need to discuss with you," said Mrs. Bluefish. She was twirling her glasses, which she could do because they were held around her neck by a small chain. "Your assignment is to report on one book, not on portions of five or six different books."

I figured this was going to be the point where she disqualified my report, but she said, "I think I might let you go ahead with this project. Strictly speaking, it doesn't fulfill the assignment I gave you, but I think you deserve some credit for the work you've put in on this."

I suppose I would have felt a little relief, but I didn't get the chance. The next thing I knew, Mrs. Bluefish had shifted into this real stern mode. She clamped her glasses down on her nose and stood up. "There is one thing I will not tolerate, however, and that is a troublemaker. What does this mean at the bottom?" she asked.

Since I couldn't see the paper, I didn't know what she was talking about.

She read it to me: "It says, 'Charly Black Crow,

AKA Floyd Rayfield.' What's the meaning of this?"

"Charly Black Crow is my chosen Sioux name," I said.

"Why do you have a chosen Sioux name? I want to know what kind of game is going on here."

"It's not a game. I know that it's my destiny to become an Indian, so I chose an appropriate name."

"What did you say?"

I repeated it: "I like to use my new name because I know it's my destiny to become an Indian. I had a vision that made it clear to me."

This got Mrs. Bluefish very uptight. She put the outline down on her desk. She clapped her hands together one time, then walked over to me in this real brisk way. She said, "You can't *become* an Indian, Floyd, you have to be *born* an Indian. If this is your idea of a joke, I suggest you think again, because I simply will not tolerate a troublemaker."

I'm used to being put down because of my belief in my destiny, but I was a little bit amazed at how excited she got. I didn't want to cause her any cardiac arrest. I was about to point out to her that I didn't fit the profile of a troublemaker, but I didn't have the energy. I asked her if I could go now so I wouldn't be late to P.E.

I guess she was all sputtered out. She said go ahead.

It didn't take long for Nicky to turn into your basic clinging vine. He started following me around like a puppy. He figured since we did time together, and since we were roommates and all, we should be friends.

We were on our way home from school one day and he said to me, "Look at this, Charly Black Crow." He started calling me Charly Black Crow after I explained to him that it was my Indian name, and my preferred name.

What he was showing me was this book on baseball lore he'd checked out of the library. He opened the book to a chapter on tricks pitchers have used throughout history to doctor the baseball. It showed all these devices used by pitchers to cut the ball, or gouge it, or scrape it, such as nails, nail files, razor blades, cheese graters, sandpaper, thumbtacks, and so forth. You couldn't use a whole cheese grater, of course, you had to use just a piece of one, something small enough that you could hide it in your mitt. The idea of cutting the ball was to make it sink when you threw it. The book had a lot of photographs of these items and how they could be hidden in a baseball glove.

Nicky showed me all of these photographs and the idiotic grin spread across his face. He said, "This is what gives you the extra edge."

What he knew was, I had agreed to play in the baseball league. I'd even given it a little thought and decided I would be a pitcher. The way baseball is played, the pitcher is the hub of the game, and everything revolves around him. The rest of the players mostly stand around bored, and get real hot in the sun, and talk to their friends, who are maybe in the game, and maybe not. Also, I happened to know that two of baseball's greatest pitchers, Chief Bender and Allie Reynolds, were Indians. That's in addition to the great Jim Thorpe, who played professional baseball but was better known for being the greatest all-around athlete in history.

I gave Nicky back his baseball book. It was just another case of his trying to make an impression by sucking up. I told him I was not all that interested in getting the extra edge, and furthermore it was not the Indian way to use illegal deception.

It didn't faze him. He just shifted gears. He said, "Do me a favor, Charly Black Crow. Come over to my mother's place, I've got something to show you that's really prime."

I didn't know what he had in mind, and I didn't really want to go to his house, but he kept pestering me about it until I agreed. Besides, I was in no particular hurry to get back to Gates House.

The truth is, going to his place really funked me out. His mother's apartment was in this run-down brick building in the sleazy part of downtown. There was an old hotel across the street, and a bar, and on another corner was a cut-rate twenty-four-hour gas station.

We had to climb a lot of stairs, because the apartment was on the third floor. The hallways were dark, there wasn't any carpeting, and the wallpaper was all peeling and water-stained.

Nicky's brother Earl was passed out in the living room on a bed that folded down out of the wall.

Earl was wearing a T-shirt and Jockey underpants.

"This is usually my bed when I'm at home," said Nicky. "Earl is just home for a little while. He works for the carnival."

Nicky was shaking Earl by the shoulders, but it was a waste of time, because Earl was out cold. I looked around the living room. There was a half-empty bottle of whiskey on the floor and several empty beer cans. There was a black banana peel with about half the banana still inside it, on the floor under the corner of the bed. Also a half-eaten sandwich right beside it, which was so old it looked like the bread had the texture of an asphalt shingle.

"I guess he's out like a light," said Nicky. "Sometimes when he gets drunk and passes out, there's no way you can wake him up."

"Where's your mother?" I said.

"She's got a second job now. She's workin' at Pizza Hut, three-thirty to eight-thirty. Right now she's just washin' dishes, but they're gonna move her up to makin' pizzas."

That was the first time I ever felt sorry for Nicky. I never did spend any time with my family or relatives in a regular house, but maybe I was better off for it. Looking at this hairball place and realizing Nicky was hung out more or less permanently between it and Gates House, I started feeling sorry for him.

It wasn't something I wanted to dwell on. "What did you want to show me?" I said.

He took me out through the kitchen door, which

went out onto the landing of the fire escape. And there it was.

It was an old Kawasaki KZ-400 street bike. It could hardly fit on the landing. "How did you get it up here?" I asked him.

"There's a freight elevator. The manager let me 'n' Earl use it."

The bike was yellow, but you could hardly tell through all the dirt and grease. The chrome had a lot of rust, and the headlight was busted. The front fender was gone, and there were spokes missing out of both wheels.

"This bike is mine." said Nicky. "Earl gave it to me to keep. It's all mine."

I took my finger and wiped some of the smear off the speedometer — 42,498 miles. If it was accurate. The front tire had highway tread, but the back was knobby tread like you'd find on a dirt bike. "What year is it?" I asked.

"It's a '74. What do you think of it?"

"It may have possibilities," I mumbled. Nicky knew that I had some experience working on engines, so I guess he wanted me to say something encouraging. "Does it run?"

"Not right now, but Earl says all it needs is a little work."

That was all I needed to hear at the moment. I told Nicky I thought we'd better get back to Gates House. He didn't want to, but then I pointed out Mrs. Grice could put us both on pro if we were later than four-thirty. He said okay, but he wanted me to stay long enough to have a Pepsi.

I sat down at the kitchen table while he scrounged around in the refrigerator. There were dirty dishes stacked all over the table, and dried food was stuck on its surface.

It turned out there wasn't any Pepsi, so he poured me some grape Hi-C. The glass he gave me was filthy. It reminded me of the ones you see the bartenders use in Westerns, where they have to blow the dust out before they pour the whiskey.

"I've been thinking," said Nicky. "I've got a bike now, right? What if we both had a bike?"

"I don't have a bike, and I don't have any plans to get one."

"But what if we did? Let's say we both had a bike, and then in the fall, when we're old enough, we get our licenses, and then we hit the road."

"Why don't you get real?"

"Just the two of us, you and me on the open road. We go all the way to Florida and lay around on sandy beaches, with lots of chicks in bikinis running around. If we needed any money, Earl could help us get a little carnival work."

I decided I couldn't stand anymore. "I'm going back," I said. "You can come with me or you can stay."

Naturally, he came with me. I was walking fast, but he was keeping up. He asked me what I thought the bike needed to get in running condition.

"I don't know, you'd have to get it in a shop somewhere to really check it out."

"Barb said I could work on it in her garage if I could get it over there."

"She did?" It gave me a little jolt hearing this, but then I figured, how likely was it that the bike would ever find its way to Barb's garage?

"I'll talk to Earl," said Nicky. "Maybe he'll help me get it over there."

"Maybe," I said.

"Then maybe sometime you 'n' me can try and get it to run."

"Maybe." This conversation didn't do too much for me because from what I could tell, Nicky didn't have much know-how when it came to engines.

Then he said, "What kind of a social worker would let you use their garage to work on your bike?"

"One that doesn't have a clue," I said.

"What's that supposed to mean?"

"She's only got four clients now, she can do what she wants. It's like a game. Let the system grind her for a while."

"I think she's real nice, Charly Black Crow."

"Of course she's nice," I said. She *was* nice, but I'd decided it wasn't a safe subject to dwell on. "I'm not talking about nice, I'm talking about experience."

He just said she was nice again. I said let's drop it.

CHAPTER SIX

The second day of the *hanblecheya* turned out to be a wholesale bummer. Actually, it was Friday, so it might have been the third day, depending on how you look at it.

Thursday went pretty well. I just mellowed out on all the Dakota history represented by my surroundings, and made notes about the time I spent at Gates House. But Friday morning after I got up, I went out of the cave and climbed up to the high ground overlook. I left my journal behind.

Up on the peak of Mount Black Elk, which was my name for this place, there was that view in front of me. As far as the eye could see, the Black Hills, and the vibes of glorious Sioux history.

But all of a sudden, I didn't feel good. I felt hungry and dizzy. I drank some of the water, but it didn't help; I just kept feeling more and more light-headed until I was real woozy.

I laid down on my back to try and make it pass. It didn't altogether pass, but I must have slept through some of it, because it wasn't until the afternoon that the bad thoughts and the bad vibes began to come.

I tried to fight it off. Here came this picture of Mrs. Bluefish: "You can't *become* an Indian, Floyd, you have to be *born* an Indian." I rolled over on the ground. Not only was I woozy, but she pissed me off. What right did she have to intrude on my *hanblecheya*?

Then I saw my conversation with Chief Bear-in-cave, in his trailer. He was telling me the story of Two-Claw and the bear that became like a pet. I rolled over again, but there was Donny Thunderbird. "A writer can do a lot of good for Indians, Floyd. A reservation is a thing of the past."

I kept trying to fight off these bad thoughts; I wanted to drive them out. But even though I was dozing in and out, sort of floating on the edge of being delirious, there was a warning in a corner of my brain: *You don't manipulate the* hanblecheya. *You take what comes*.

The chief summed up the meaning of the Two-Claw story: "It's a lot like that when you're an Indian on a reservation."

Donny Thunderbird: "A reservation is a thing of the past."

Mrs. Bluefish: "You can't *become* an Indian, Floyd, you have to be *born* an Indian."

I kept rolling over, right and left. It was like a conspiracy, the way these same words and pictures kept busting into my brain. I saw myself the first day I got to the reservation; I was walking around the campground picking up Pepsi cans and Styro-foam cups. What did I think I was going to do, live on the reservation and pick up litter for the rest of my life?

I don't know how long the bad vibes package lasted. Over and over, the same pictures and the same words. I was semiconscious part of the time, half asleep. When I was conscious, I was like partly delirious. There wasn't any sense of time to it.

By the time I came out of it, more or less, it was close to dusk. I was like a person who breaks a long fever; I was shaky and clammy, but I wasn't woozy anymore, and I had my faculties.

I only wished I didn't. I sat up against the base of this shaggy pine tree, and the meaning of things was real clear to me. A lot clearer than I wanted.

The truth was, there wasn't any destiny. There never had been. What I had, instead of a destiny, was a colorful fantasy, the kind that crazies create in their peculiar little minds when they can't deal with the world the way it really is.

It was real bitter, but it was a conclusion I didn't try to fight off. In their kind and gentle way, that was the point that Donny and the chief had tried to make to me. Way back when, when I was just a kid, I felt real close to the Indians because their situation seemed just like mine. They kept getting jerked around all the time, from their lands and places, when all they wanted was to be left alone to live their lives in peace. That's all they wanted, that's all I wanted.

I felt so clammy, I started to get the shakes. Since I wasn't dizzy or anything like that, I climbed down to the cave and got my denim jacket. Then back up to the tree trunk.

I was cold and naked and alone. The only company I had was the awful truth, and I couldn't stop thinking about it. My destiny had been manufactured by my brain to make up for all those years of being bounced around from one placement to another. In the looney bin they call it compensation, or if you're really off-the-wall, a delusion. Maybe I was just as looney as Mrs. Bluefish thought I was.

I was so lonely all of a sudden. There were even tears running down my face. I didn't want to stay anymore; I wanted to go back to the reservation. I had my vision, the truth was revealed to me, and now I was all hollow inside. What would be the point in staying any longer?

I think I would have gone back, only it was after dark and I was too shaky. I didn't like my chances of making it without falling off a cliff or something. The blessing was sleep. I was so exhausted, I fell asleep right there on the clearing.

When I woke up the next morning, I was resigned; it was a different head, a sort of neutral zone, like a return to numb-out. I decided to go ahead and stick out the rest of the vision quest. Or to tell the truth, I decided not to do anything. I drank some water and went back to my journal.

At Gates House, the situation was about to get worse. Not that I could see it coming. Nicky's Kawasaki got moved to Barb's garage. I don't know how, but somehow Nicky got his brother Earl sobered up and the two of them got their asses in gear long enough to transport it.

It was not a situation I was keen on, because it just gave Nicky all the more reason to cling. He was such a pest about it that after a couple of days, I finally agreed to go over there with him to see if we could get it running.

We had to use the sign-out sheet because we had to walk, and it's over a mile to Barb's house. Nicky said to me, "You took the X off again, didn't you?"

"I plead the Fifth Amendment."

"Don't bullshit me, you took it off. You're gonna get your ass in a sling."

"It's my ass."

"How'd you get it off?"

I had to laugh. "She's making it tougher, now she uses strapping tape. I had to use a putty knife."

"It's pretty risky, how come you keep doing it?"

"It's the principle of the thing."

"I don't get it."

I said, "You take a slimeball like Mrs. Grice. Her power trip is dumping on poor slobs like Kinderhook. It's too easy. You see what I mean, it's the principle of the thing."

"You got balls, Charly Black Crow, but you're gonna get your ass in a sling."

When we got to Barb's house, she was on the

phone; she motioned us to get some pop from the fridge. After Nicky got us both a Pepsi, we went out to the garage.

We looked over the filthy bike. "The first thing that's obvious," I said, "is that everything will have to be cleaned."

"I'm with you, Charly Black Crow."

"I really doubt if you are. I'm not just talking about the dirt you can see, I'm talking about really cleaning this machine up. It needs everything pulled apart and cleaned with gasoline, and I mean everything — plugs, points, and carburetors, filters, even the fuel line."

"Let's do it, partner."

We were in good shape for tools, thanks to Barb's dead husband. I took the air filter off of the bike and we set it on the workbench. "This'll show you why it's going to be such a big job," I said. "All we can do with this is brush it out. It ought to be blown out with a compressor, but we don't have one. Even that would be just a temporary solution. What it really needs is a new air filter, which means money."

"I can get a new one later," said Nicky.

"Just remember, there's no way to get this bike running good without spending some money." I didn't want to be stiff with him, but there wasn't any point in hiding from the truth.

We took the gas tank off, which wasn't too tricky. I gave Nicky some gas and a stiff old paintbrush. "Why don't you see if you can get that grease and crud off the gas tank," I said. "I'll work on this filter for a while."

After he worked on it for about two minutes, he told me he was done. I looked at it, but all he'd done was smear off some of the crud from the top of the tank. I got pissed and jumped on his case. I told him if he didn't care enough to do a good job, why should I care?

He said okay, but first he had to go to the bathroom.

Just after he went out, Barb came in. She hung a key on a nail next to the workbench. "This is in case you need to get in the house," she said. "I'm going out to Nolan's house for a while."

"Have a good time."

"Speaking of Nolan," she said, "have you been working on your curveball?"

"Night and day," I lied. "If we ever get this bike running, I'll probably be working out even more."

"How did you get roped in?" she asked.

"A certain lady we know made her garage and her tools available."

"Aha. Are you mad at me?"

"Not really. It's just that Nicky's such a clinging vine. If you show him any encouragement, he'll wrap himself around you. He doesn't have enough know-how to work on the bike himself; as long as it's in this garage, he's going to want me to help him work on it, and that'll turn out to be me doing most of the work."

"I never thought of that. I just felt sorry for him

because he doesn't seem to have much going for himself."

"He doesn't know how to get anything going. He's very pathetic, as you'll find out in due time."

Then I thought I sounded like a big whining baby.

"I never thought how it might affect you," she repeated. "I can understand your point."

I could tell how sincere she was, which made it worse. I felt like a jerk. "Never mind. It would be worse feeling guilty and self-centered than having him clinging around."

We dropped the subject and she took off in the station wagon. After Nicky came out back, we worked on the bike for maybe two hours. We cleaned the plugs and sprayed out the inside of both carburetors with gum-out.

The net result was, we got it running, for about twenty minutes. It was running real rough and burning oil, but we drove it to the orchard on the other side of Birkelbaw's garden market. We both got to drive a little bit.

On the way back, it conked out several blocks from Barb's house. We tried for quite a while, but we couldn't get it started again. Nicky pushed it over on its side and started kicking it.

I was completely disgusted with him. "I tried to tell you how much work it would be to get it running right. There's a lot more to it than we did today."

He just kept kicking the bike. I couldn't see any reason to be polite to him. I didn't lift a finger to help him, I let him walk it back by himself.

After that, he was in a heavy-duty sulk all the way home.

One day during the last few weeks of school, I had my story finished for the competition, so I turned it in to Mrs. Bluefish. The idea was, you were supposed to turn your story in to your English teacher and then the teachers would send the stories on to the contest judges. Probably the plan was to have the teachers weed out some of the stories that were real losers. The actual judging was going to be done during summer vacation.

The name of my story was "Mask." I worked pretty hard on it, and typed it all up with no typos. It was a quality piece of work, if I do say so myself. The story line went like this: There's this guy named Glenn Carbon who wears this mask all the time, everywhere he goes. He's a computer programmer in a big company. The mask is one of those rubbery types that fits very snug over your whole head and even covers part of your neck. When Glenn Carbon was in high school, he only wore the mask part of the time, but now he wears it all the time. He wears it to work, he wears it when he goes shopping, and he even wears it to bed, because if he gets a phone call, he wants to have the mask on when he's talking on the phone.

Even though he has this one weird trait, he is very excellent at his job.

One day the company has an office party, and Glenn Carbon gets drunk. He gets so drunk, he passes out. Well, everyone else is drunk, too, so while he's passed out, the other people decide they will take off his mask to see what his face looks like. They discover that his real face looks exactly like the mask. In fact, you have to look real close to be certain that he's not still wearing it. Well, this seems close enough to the edge that it sobers everybody up. When Glenn Carbon comes to, he discovers that his mask is gone. He freaks out and starts throwing computers out the window. Nobody can quite understand the freak-out, because his face actually looks the same, with or without the mask. But he can't handle it, so the authorities come and take him away to a mental institution, where he lives out the rest of his days in a catatonic condition.

When I handed in the story to Mrs. Bluefish, she kept this stern expression on her face and said, "Thank you, Floyd. I hope you've written a nice story." She seemed her usual edgy self, as you could see her jaw muscles working.

What she meant by a *nice story* is the kind Annette Belfoglio always turns in, where this Red Cross nurse takes care of a wounded soldier, they fall in love in the hospital, and after the war is over they get married. Sometimes Annette changes the details a little bit; instead of a Red Cross nurse, it is a nurse in a city hospital, and instead of a wounded soldier, the man is a policeman or a fireman injured in the line of duty.

After school, Nicky wanted to know if we could go back to the garage and try to get the bike running again. With my story finished and handed in, I was feeling altogether mellow, so I said yes.

When we got to Barb's house, she wasn't home. It didn't seem like she'd mind if we did a little work anyhow, so we went around back. In the backyard, I had to do a doubletake.

On the ground between the house and the garage was a huge log with a blue ribbon tied around the middle of it. I read the card that was attached to the blue ribbon:

> I got the log, now
> you make the boat.

"What's the story?" asked Nicky.

I was impressed with how straight and regular the log was. I told Nicky, "Sometimes Barb and I talk about Indian customs. I showed her this book once with pictures of the steps involved in making a dug-out canoe."

"So?"

"So, I told her I'd like to make one sometime." I got a tape measure from the garage and measured the log. It was fourteen feet long, and thirty inches in diameter. It was well seasoned, but it didn't have any rotten spots. As near as I could tell, it was cottonwood.

I tried to remember when anyone had done anything this nice for me, anything that took so much extra effort. Maybe the time Mr. Gibbs gave me a rebuilt lawn mower engine to tinker on. Maybe not.

Maybe never. But I knew for sure it wasn't the kind of thing you could let yourself dwell on.

"If you're gonna make a boat out of this thing, you're lookin' at a lot of work," said Nicky.

"True, but the log couldn't be any more perfect. I wonder where she got it."

"What's the big deal? If you want a log, you cut down a tree."

"It's not that simple. Not to get a log with all the right elements. Her friend Nolan, the baseball coach who lives on the farm, she probably got it from him. He lives out in the country and he would have a truck to haul it."

"If you say so." Nicky seemed bored. He got Barb's house key from the garage and asked me if I wanted a Pepsi.

"Maybe we shouldn't go inside when she's not home."

"She left us a key, right? She showed us where she keeps it."

He came back out with two Pepsis. He started pestering me to go to work on the motorcycle. I apologized for going back on my word, but I told him I hadn't known the log would be here, and I really wanted to start working on it. I told him he could work on the bike for a while by himself. "If you run into anything that's tricky, like over your head, I'll give you a hand."

That seemed to satisfy him. He went to the garage.

Since it was just me and the log now, I had to do

a little brainstorming. There was a long crack down one side of the log, sort of like a natural seam. I needed some wide chisels and a sledgehammer, but I was in luck because I knew the stuff was in the garage.

When I went in there, Nicky wasn't working on his bike at all. He was sitting on it. He was wearing a baseball cap turned around, and humming "Born to Be Wild." There was no telling what pictures were in his brain.

I shook my head and got the tools. I started to work. I wasn't at it too long when I saw Nicky out of the corner of my eye. He was leaving.

I ended up working on the log right up until dark. Barb got home about 5:30 and asked me if I wanted some supper.

"No, thanks, I'm on a roll. I really appreciate the log, though. It's real nice of you."

"You're welcome."

"Would you do me a favor and call Gates House? I have to have permission to stay past supper."

When she came back out of the house, she had a bag of pretzels. "I've been on the phone with Mrs. Grice."

"What'd she say?"

"She said yes, but she wanted to say no. She's a woman without much enthusiasm, I'd say." It was a little hard to understand Barb, with her mouth full.

"That's putting it mildly."

"You, on the other hand, are a person with lots of enthusiasm."

"Is that how you see it?"

"Well, just look at yourself. Sweating like a dog and ready to go another couple of hours."

"This is pure pleasure," I said. "What could be more authentic to the Indian way of life than a hand-made dugout canoe?"

She said, "If that's not enthusiasm I don't know what is."

On the way home from school, Tuesday, Nicky wanted to know if he could help me with the boat. I suppose he figured the sooner the canoe was finished, the sooner I'd help him work on the bike again. I said okay, even though it was a project I'd definitely have preferred to do alone.

We walked over to Barb's. As soon as we got there, I gave Nicky one of the chisels and a regular hammer. We chiseled at it until the trench was opened up pretty good. Nicky kept telling me we ought to be using the chain saw.

"Did you ever use a chain saw?"

"No."

"Did you ever hear of an Indian using a chain saw?"

"Okay, okay."

"It doesn't matter," I said. "It's time to burn this trench."

"Burn it?"

"That's how it was always done by the Northern

tribes. When you get it opened up like this, you can burn it. It makes the trench bigger, and it softens it up for easier chiseling."

Nicky liked the sound of this step, I guess, because it seemed like it was going to be a lot less work. He went to the garage while I went to the basement. I figured he was going to gaze at his motorcycle for a while.

My plan was to line the trench of the log with shredded newspapers, to get the fire going, so I was searching through some stacks of newspaper in the corner, looking for the dry ones. Most of them were damp, so I must have been there ten or fifteen minutes before I had enough. That turned out to be a big mistake.

I was just starting back up the basement stairs, when, through the back door, I saw this enormous cloud of black smoke pouring up into the sky. I went into a sort of panic and ran out as fast as I could. The whole log was engulfed in blue and yellow flames; it was sending up the sort of black smoke you get from a fire in a refinery. Nicky was slapping at the fire with a throw rug.

I got another throw rug and the two of us slapped at it, but it was an incredible blaze; you couldn't believe how hot it was. It was singeing some low-hanging leaves, and there were even some small flames on the tips of the evergreen shrubs.

There's no way I'm a violent person, but about the time I first heard the siren of the fire engine, I took Nicky by his motorcycle jacket and made him tell me what happened. He said it was a little gas-oline, some fuel oil, and a couple cans of charcoal starter; he'd gotten them all from the garage. He also said he was sorry, he was only trying to help.

The firemen showed up in this gigantic truck, and they hosed out the flaming log in no time. Now the log was soaking wet and had that stinking, charred smell you get when a wood fire is put out with water. The backyard looked like a swamp, and I felt like a jerk. I don't know how many people were hanging around on the sidewalk and staring.

A fireman named Weatherwax, who acted like he was the honcho, started going through the house. He was carrying an ax. I kept telling him that there wasn't any fire except the log, and I also told him in a polite way that he shouldn't be going through the house. He kept asking me, "Who's in charge here?"

I explained to Weatherwax about three times that Barb was our social worker. "We have permission to be here. You can call her and ask her."

It didn't cut any mustard. Weatherwax was the type who is all business, all hung up on his authority. He finally went into the backyard again and stared at the log, which wasn't even smoldering. He de-manded to know what was the meaning of this.

I told him I was using the log to make a dugout canoe.

"A what?"

"A dugout canoe," I said.

"A what?" Then he said, "There will be a full

report on this, boys." Before he left, he told Nicky to get a haircut.

After they had gone, Nicky apologized approximately two dozen times. I finally told him to just shut up. I couldn't stand any more apologies, and all the people staring at us were making me tense. I inspected the log real carefully, and to my relief there wasn't much damage. It would take about two eons for it to dry out, but the wood itself wasn't burned much at all. It could have been a lot worse.

CHAPTER SEVEN

As soon as Mrs. Grice found out about the log fiasco, we both went on pro again. Strict pro this time, with no privileges at all.

Barb had a talk with Mrs. Grice, but she couldn't even get the probation shortened. In my opinion, she was just getting herself into no-man's-land by thinking she could buck the system, or at least bend it her way.

It was the Thursday of the last week of school, just before Memorial Day weekend. Most people were taking final exams, but I was catching a break; I only had to take unit tests since I'd just been in school a couple of months.

Anyway, Mrs. Bluefish said I had to go see Mr. Saberhagen again. She didn't give me any reason, she just said I was supposed to go to his office.

He put me in a chair at the front of his desk and said in his formal voice, "Floyd, something quite serious has come up, which we need to discuss."

I told him I was listening. I was still wearing my

moccasins, so I figured he was about to get on my case about that again.

Mr. Saberhagen seemed a little stressed; he was playing with the knot on his necktie and doing even more neck stretching than usual. Then he said, "Floyd, let me come right to the point. Mrs. Bluefish and I have both read the story you submitted for the young authors' competition. We think it's very disturbing. We don't question your interest in writing, and we don't doubt your talent, but it is our decision to withdraw this story from the competition."

I was stunned. Was he talking about "Mask"?

Mr. Saberhagen continued, "A young man with your ability ought to be able to write a ripsnorting tale of adventure and excitement. But this story is very disturbing. It's what I would call psychologically irregular."

"Psychologically irregular?"

"Yes. It seems abnormal, to be blunt about it. Your mind seems to be moving in some very murky waters. Mrs. Bluefish tells me this is not the first time you have turned in this kind of work."

"When I write stories, I like to use my imagination."

"Imagination is fine, Floyd, but there is imagination, and then there is such a thing as preoccupation with unhealthy thoughts. Believe me, I get no pleasure in telling you this, but our decision to withdraw the story has to be final."

I was still stunned. "What you're saying is, I'm insane."

Then he took off on this long speech about how nobody was saying I was exactly insane, and so on and so forth. I didn't hear most of what he was saying because I was going into a very deep funk. I was plenty pissed, to tell the truth. All the time he was talking, I was staring at his paperweight, which was a glass sphere about the size of a baseball. It was one of those types that has a snowman in it, and if you turn it upside down it gets filled with snow-flakes. I felt like picking it up and throwing it through the wall behind him, which was all dark plate glass, with secretaries on the other side. I pictured the paperweight smashing all the glass to smithereens and these little fragments of broken glass whizzing around the room.

The problem is, you can get pissed about things that happen, but all it usually means is you end up bashing your head against the wall. Then you get in trouble, so you get even more pissed, which means it just goes on and on.

Saberhagen said, "Maybe you'd like to try and submit another story. Maybe you could come up with something a little more wholesome."

"What, in two days?"

"I know it's discouraging. And as I said, we don't think you're insane, but we do think it might be a good idea if you had a few talks with Mrs. Lacey."

Mrs. Lacey is the agency psychologist. I didn't really know her. I was tired of the whole conversation, anyway, and I just wanted to leave. I asked Saberhagen if that was all.

He said I could go. As I was leaving, he said he was sorry.

Not half as sorry as I was. I went home in a wholesale funk. As soon as I got to my room, Kinderhook started hanging around. He was talking about television, but I wasn't listening.

I decided to go to the park, just to get away from everything and everybody. Kinderhook wanted to come along, but I said no. I slipped out through the fire escape. Of course being on pro, it was illegal for me to leave the house, but I didn't give a shit.

I stayed in the park for over two hours. I wrote some things in my journal, mostly thoughts about making peace with life and living your own way. I gave some serious thought to taking off. I could pack my few important belongings and make my way to the appropriate reservation, where I could begin my real life as a Sioux. I would be in a different universe practically, a universe where my own ideals would fit in with the ideals of the group, and Mrs. Grice and Mr. Saberhagen and Mrs. Bluefish would have no authority over me.

By the time I got back to Gates House, everybody was about to sit down for dinner.

Afterward, it was my night for garbage detail. On my way back in from the Dumpster, I walked into the lounge where right away I saw Nicky and Slive, squared off. They were right in front of the TV.

Nicky was saying to Slive, "You wanna fight somebody so bad, you try me out."

"Are you crazy?" said Slive. "You just don't want to keep your teeth, or what?"

Kinderhook was sitting on the couch, staring at them. I figured he was in the middle of it somehow with his pitiful TV hang-ups, but I knew sooner or later Nicky would get into it with Slive. He just had to.

I kept watching them while I put the garbage can back under the sink. Nicky took a swing at Slive but missed. Slive hit him in the mouth and knocked him down. Then he kicked him in the back.

I'm not sure what happened to me, but the next thing I knew, I was hitting Slive in the side of the head with my fist. I didn't realize how hard I hit him; he fell over into the corner and knocked a planter down. Nicky was all over Slive in the corner, punching him in the head while he was down.

I ended up trying to pull Nicky off him. Mrs. Grice was suddenly in the room, yelling at the top of her lungs, and Marty was breaking up the fight.

Mrs. Grice chased everyone else out of the room except the three of us, and then she made us sit down far apart from each other. Marty tried to set the planter back into a standing position, but it was too busted up. There was potting soil all over the place, even on the furniture.

I was the only one with no physical damage. About all I needed to do to recover was catch my breath and rub my sore hand. All of Nicky's hair was in his face. His mouth was full of blood, and it looked like he had at least one tooth missing. His lips were already swelled up.

Slive had blood coming out of his eyebrow on one side, and his other eye was a big red welt.

We all kept our faces down while Mrs. Grice read us the riot act for a long time. I don't think anyone was paying attention, I know I wasn't. When she finished her speech, she looked at me and said: "Floyd, you get on the X."

I didn't even have to think about it. I looked straight at her and said, "I'm not getting on the X."

"What did you say to me?"

"I said I'm not getting on the X."

I guess Mrs. Grice had never been spoken to like that before. You could have heard a pin drop. Her loose lips were just hanging there. Out of the corner of my eye, I saw Slive blow his nose and get a handful of blood. There was blood dripping from Nicky's mouth onto the floor.

Mrs. Grice was practically sputtering. She said, "Are you defying me?"

"I guess I am."

"You think you're innocent in this situation?"

"I didn't say that. I just said I'm not getting on the X."

Then Marty said, "Better do as she says, Floyd."

I looked right at him. "If anybody ever wants me on that X, they're going to have to tie me down. That's the only way I'll be there." Then I looked at

Mrs. Grice again. I said to her, "By the way, that's a tone of voice."

I just couldn't resist saying it. The funny part was, I was thinking more about my story than I was about the fight.

There must have been a look on my face to go with the tone in my voice, because Marty went into private whispering with Mrs. Grice. It was Marty doing most of the talking; Mrs. Grice was still more or less speechless.

The decision they reached was for me to go to my room and stay there while Marty took Nicky and Slive for medical attention.

The next morning, when I had my breakfast and went to school with no one saying a word, I thought the whole thing might blow over. But when I got home in the afternoon, that psychologist, Mrs. Lacey, and Mr. Wagner were sitting in the lounge with Mrs. Grice. Mr. Wagner is the head of the agency.

They said they wanted to talk to me. I knew it was about to hit the fan big-time.

Mr. Wagner laid a Ziploc bag of brown shredded stuff on the coffee table. It was my willow bark. "Maybe you could start by telling us what this is," he said.

I couldn't believe it. "That was in my dresser drawer," I said. "You got in my stuff."

"The way things have been developing, we thought some searching was justified," said Mr. Wagner. "We don't like to do it any more often than we have to. Yours was not the only room searched, I might add."

"That's supposed to make me feel better?"

"Let's return to the question. Can you tell us what's in this bag?"

"It's willow bark," I said. "I got it from the park."

Mrs. Lacey was making notes. The next thing I knew, Mr. Wagner was setting my ceremonial pipe next to the Ziploc bag. "And this?"

I told him it was my Dakota ceremonial pipe. This was really funking me out. When people go through your stuff, it makes you feel like you've been betrayed.

Mrs. Lacey said, "The pipe is a ceremonial Indian pipe, and the substance is willow bark?"

"That's what I said. This is comical, because you think you've found some hash or grass."

"We don't know what we've found," said Mrs. Lacey, "but we soon will."

Mr. Wagner said, "We'll have it tested. I'd like to believe it's just willow bark you picked up in the park, but that does sound a little farfetched, doesn't it?"

"Not to me. Not if you hold Indian ways in high esteem the way I do."

"Do you smoke the bark in this pipe?" asked Mrs. Lacey.

"Sometimes."

"Why?"

"The Plains Indians, especially the Dakota, smoke willow bark in their ceremonials on special occasions. It's very solemn; it's like a ritual. It doesn't make you high or anything. Getting high is not the point."

Mrs. Grice was just sitting there staring at me, not saying a word, but with a self-satisfied look on her face.

I guess Mr. Wagner was getting a little impatient. He said, "In any case, we'll have it tested and then we'll know. In the meantime, Floyd, we'd like you to pack a few things. We're going to have you spend a little time at The Elms for testing and evaluation."

"You're telling me what?"

"It may turn out that we can do all the evaluation we need over the weekend, in which case you would be back home by the first of the week."

"The Elms is the looney bin," I said. "You think I'm insane or something."

"That's not exactly the point," said Mrs. Lacey. "But much of your behavior has been inappropriate, and we think some thorough testing would be advisable."

"I've got willow bark in my room so I get put in the looney bin?"

Mrs. Grice said, "That's the tone of voice he uses."

Mr. Wagner put up his hand, the way an orchestra conductor does. He was polished and slick, he was like oil. He said, "It isn't just the substance, Floyd, it's a pattern of inappropriate behavior. Yesterday, you were fighting and you were defiant with Mrs. Grice. Apparently you've been defiant at school as well."

Mrs. Lacey said, "You've only lived at Gates House for two months and yet you've been on probation twice."

This was nuts. I had this hollow feeling in the pit of my stomach. Helpless. I could have said something else, but what's the point with the deck stacked?

Mrs. Lacey said, "Maybe it will help if you try not to think of this as punishment."

"Right," I said.

She went on, "Psychological evaluation is meant to help us learn things about ourselves so we can make better decisions."

"That's a good point," said Mr. Wagner. "Try to think of this as a learning experience. What we really want to do is help you, Floyd."

I felt like I'd had the wind knocked out of me. "Right," I said again.

The next thing I knew I was in the van with my small suitcase between me and Marty, who was doing the driving. Everything seemed to be going so fast, it was making me numb.

I turned to Marty. "You think this is right?"

"They're not locking you up, Floyd. It's just temporary, for evaluation."

"But what I said was, do you think this is right?"

"It's not my job to make these kinds of decisions."

Perfect, I thought.

The Elms is the psycho wing of the county hospital. Marty was sitting with me in a small, bare room until a lady named Mrs. Greene came in. She had a clipboard and some folders. She introduced herself and told us she was a psychiatric social worker.

The first thing she asked me was my name, and I said, "Charly Black Crow."

She looked at me, and so did Marty. He had the look on his face of someone trying to be patient. "Don't start, Floyd. This doesn't have to be difficult."

"Whatever," I said.

She asked me again, and I told her Floyd Rayfield. She wanted me to spell it, so I did that, too. After that, Marty left.

Mrs. Greene had a whole slew of questions, but it didn't take her long to get around to drugs. She wanted to know what the substance was they had found in my room. I repeated all the same stuff I had told Mr. Wagner and Mrs Lacey.

She said, "You collect willow bark, from a park, and you smoke it in an Indian pipe, but only on solemn occasions."

"Right."

"And what would constitute such a solemn occasion?"

"For one example, a Dakota smokes it if he's about to begin a vision seek. For another example, they smoke it when they make important decisions."

She looked up from the clipboard. "We'll wait for lab results on the substance."

"The lab results will tell you the same thing I'm saying."

She looked down at the clipboard again. Her questions must have come from a checklist, the way she asked them so fast. "Floyd, do you ever use any drugs?"

"No."

"Do you ever use any alcohol?"

"No."

"Have you used any drugs or alcohol within the past month?"

"No drugs and no alcohol."

"What do you think about drugs? I'm talking about the kind that are often used by teenagers."

"If you use drugs, you don't see things clearly. The Dakota never use drugs." Unfortunately a lot of them are alcoholics, but why should I mention that to her?

She changed the subject. "Have you received any blow to the head within the past month?"

"No."

"Be sure before you answer. Have you had a fall that might have caused you to bump your head?"

"No."

"Have you been in good health for the past month?"

"Yes."

"How do you feel now?"

What was I supposed to say to that? "Physically, I feel fine. Mentally, I can't believe I'm even here."

Mrs. Greene looked at me, but she didn't say anything.

I said to her, "Are you keeping me in this place? Do you think I'm insane?"

"Mrs. Lacey thinks it would be a good idea to keep you here for a little while, for evaluation. I agree with her. We'd like to do some tests while you're here. We aren't judging you."

"How long is a little while?"

"Probably only for a few days," said Mrs. Greene.

Then she took me up to the second floor, to my room. In some ways it looked like a hospital room, but in others it seemed like a motel. The twin beds weren't the hospital type. There was no TV, but there was a desk. One wall was made up of built-in closets, called bolsters. Mrs. Greene told me there was a roommate, named Gary, but he was gone at the moment.

"Gone where?" I said.

"I think he's in group therapy," she said. "We have programming most of the day, and some programming in the evenings as well."

Then she told me I would be assigned a nurse; the nurse would be coming soon to unlock the bolster so I could put my things away.

If I thought it was hard talking to Nicky or Kinderhook, I realized how mistaken I'd been when I met my hospital roommate, the guy named Gary.

When he came into the room, he started peering inside the lamp shades. He unscrewed the light bulbs and inspected them like a jeweler looking at a ring.

"These rooms are usually bugged," he said.

He looked like he was a couple years older than me, maybe seventeen or eighteen. He sat down on the other bed. He was tall and thin, with a real short haircut that looked like a chop job, like he'd cut it himself or had a friend do it.

I had the feeling if I tried to have a conversation with him, it would end up going nowhere, but I asked him why the rooms were bugged.

"The hospital staff bugs the rooms so they can get information on you. They use it against you later on. If they can hear the things you say in private, then they've got something on you they can use."

Not that I believed what he was saying, but I had the feeling he couldn't handle it if you disagreed with him. "Why do they snoop on the things you say?" I asked.

"Because of the quota they have to maintain. There has to be a certain number of crazy people."

I said, "I think maybe your imagination is running a little wild."

"Look," he said. "Do anything you want, but don't call me paranoid."

"I'm not calling you anything. Why are you telling me all this?"

"I'm trying to give you the benefit of my expertise. The staff here has a quota to maintain. Not enough crazy people, and they're out of a job. Think about it. It's like the state cops. If they don't get a certain

number of speeders, they're gonna be out of a job.
It's the same principle here. They'll trap you any
way they can. Take my advice and don't cooperate."

He was getting on my nerves. "Let me tell you
something," I said. "I don't have anything to hide.
There's nothing wrong with my mind. I'm not afraid
of their questions and I'm not afraid of my answers.
And don't take everything so personal."

He stood up with this real injured look on his
face. "I probably shouldn't even be talking to you,
you're probably a plant or a spy. All I'm trying to
do here is give you some good advice, but if you
don't want it, it's no skin off mine." He went into
the bathroom.

He was a trip. I was on edge from trying to talk
to him. After lights out, I waited until he was asleep.
Then I took a blanket and a pillow down to the
lounge and went to sleep stretched out in a recliner.

I decided I would ask Mrs. Greene to get me
another roommate. Then I decided to tell Mrs.
Greene I didn't belong here, and I wanted out.
I couldn't help but wonder where Barb was; she
hadn't contacted me. Maybe she was whipped —
maybe she was finally getting the point that the
system is something you just can't beat.

It was a thought that funked me out. It was a long
time before I finally went to sleep.

CHAPTER EIGHT

I spent most of my first full day at The Elms getting tested. Several of the tests were physical, such as certain neurological tests and some blood tests.

But most of the tests were mental. A lot of them were the ordinary stuff you might expect; you just looked at pictures of inkblots and told what you saw, and drew some pictures, and answered a lot of questions. I kept answering questions about my willow bark and my ceremonial. But each time I answered, someone would start asking me about drugs. They kept asking me about drugs and blows to my head; in a place like this, you get interviewed by so many people that you keep answering the same questions over and over.

When they assigned me to do a mental test called the *ring sort*, they put me right next to Gary, at the same table. That was not a pleasant situation, so I moved my chair down close to the end. The ring sort is a test where you have to arrange different sized rings on these vertical rods. And you're supposed to arrange them in a certain order so they form pyramids. I think it's a test of frustration level.

Right after supper, Barb came. I felt some relief, even though it was obvious she didn't; she had that hassled look.

"I just found out this afternoon. We had a staffing on you."

"You've got a lot of stuff," I said. I meant all the folders and notebooks she was carrying.

"It was a long staffing, more than two hours."

"Who was there?"

"Just about everyone in the world. Wagner, Lacey, Mrs. Grice. Your assistant principal was even there."

"Saberhagen? What for?"

"He was there to testify that you're psychologically irregular."

"That's the label they put on my story. They took my story out of the competition."

"I know. We spent a lot of time talking about that."

I said to her, "That really bummed me out."

"I haven't read your story, but I've read *Frankenstein* and *Dr. Jekyll and Mr. Hyde*. I pointed out that those stories are probably psychologically irregular, as well."

"You told them that?"

"We went around about it. I told them that the real issue should be whether the story is well written. I also pointed out that since the school isn't actually the sponsor of the contest, they're really overstepping their authority."

I knew Barb had a real temper, and a short fuse. I only wished I could have been there to see her chew ass on Saberhagen.

Then she looked at me and changed the subject. "You've been a naughty boy, though."

I asked her what she meant by that.

"You took Mrs. Grice's X off the floor. More than once."

"The X is cruel and unusual punishment. If you were ever one of the poor bastards who had to stand on it, you'd know what I mean."

"So you took it off as a matter of principle."

"You could put it that way."

"Floyd, there are ways of doing things. People can help you."

This again, I thought. "Not when it comes to the system," I said. "When it comes to the system, either you get on board or you get flushed out. You talk to me about standing up for your rights. I tried that with Saberhagen when they withdrew my story. I tried it with Wagner — I told him it wasn't right for them to search my things. Where did all this standing up get me? It got me here. In the puzzle house."

"I know."

"You even tried it yourself when you wanted to get my probation reduced."

"I have not yet begun to fight. Speaking of which, what happened with you and Nicky in the lounge?"

"I was just pissed about the story. I more or less flipped out and then I hit Slive in the head. Right after that I was trying to break it up."

Barb stood up. "Let's go downstairs."

We went down to the lounge, where there were vending machines. She got a bag of Cajun Spice Ruffles and started crunching. "You left Gates House several times when you were on probation."

This was starting to annoy me. Especially coming from her. It must have told on my face because she said, "Look, Floyd, I spent the afternoon hearing all of these charges against you. Now I'd like to hear your side of things."

"It's true. I was sneaking out the fire escape."

"Where were you going?"

"No place in particular. Either the park or the library. I was doing research for a report in English class. Mostly it was just to get away from Gates House and Mrs. Grice, or to get away from Nicky and Kinderhook and all their clinging."

"That's about what I figured. Still, it wasn't the best way to go about it."

I said to her, "Do you think I belong here or what?"

"Of course not. I'm trying to get you out."

"What else went on at the staffing?"

"If I tell you, it's going to get you down."

"Tell me anyway. I think I have a right to know. You're always big on rights."

So she summed up the other stuff that had come up. The log catching fire was big. It was brought up that I wrote weird stories. It was brought up that I'm intractable and defiant; my moccasins were part

137

of the evidence. Then she added, "There was a letter from Mrs. Bluefish and another one from Reverend Braithwaite. Mrs. Bluefish wrote that since you really and truly believe you're going to be an Indian someday, it shows you're psychologically disturbed. Reverend Braithwaite's letter said you need proper religious training."

I said, "I wear Dakota moccasins to school and told the reverend about some Indian miracles. Now I'm in the looney bin. You see how nuts that sounds?"

"I warned you this would get you down, but you had to know."

"Right. I had to know."

"Let's go outside."

We went out to this patio, which was somewhat like a sunken courtyard, so Barb could light up. She said, "We talked about a new placement."

"Naturally."

"You don't like it at Gates House. Why wouldn't you like to talk about a new placement?"

The more we talked about these things, the more depressing it seemed. "I told you once, I hate getting hung out all the time. I was hung out most of this year, up until April. Besides, if Wagner and those other agency honchos have their way, they'll just get me placed in one of those hard-core houses like The Tunnels."

"That sounds like you're anticipating the worst."

"I'd be an idiot to anticipate anything else. You

were the one at the staffing. If that wasn't a hatchet job, then what was it?"

Barb tried to blow a smoke ring, but there was too much wind. She said, "I'd like to try to find you a good placement in a foster home. One like you had with Mr. and Mrs. Gibbs. That's what I'd like to work on. Are you interested?"

"I don't know. I can put in my time at Gates House if I have to."

She said, "Maybe you don't have to. Do me a favor and think it over. I have to go to Missouri tomorrow for a wedding in Nolan's family. I'm going to be out of town for a couple of days."

"I'll be here when you get back."

"I hope you won't be. I'm pushing for you to be dismissed. We can talk about it after I get back, when you've had some time to think it over. Unless of course you don't want to; I'm not going to force you to talk about a new placement if you don't want to."

Just about that time, a nurse came out. She said there was a group therapy I had to go to, so Barb said good-bye. She told me to keep my chin up. "I'll see you when I get back."

The next day, I was reading a book in leisure time. Gary came up and wanted to talk. He wanted to know what I was in for.

"It's hard to say," I said. "It was a combination of little things. They had a way of adding up that didn't make sense."

"Such as?"

I told him about the fight and the pipe and the willow bark. I didn't go into the log, or my moccasins, et cetera.

"My friend, you've been railroaded."

I told him about Mrs. Grice, and how I refused to stand on the X when she told me to.

"I'd say you did the right thing," said Gary. "She sounds like a dead solid hairbag."

Then I tried to get back to my reading because I hoped the conversation was over. But no way. Gary started explaining what he was in for. It turned out he'd burned down his neighbor's garage. "I have to go to trial for it next month," he said.

So I asked him why he torched the garage.

"It was because of my pheasant," he said.

I had no idea what he was talking about, but he just went right on with the story.

"See, I have this pheasant stuffed and mounted on the wall in my bedroom. It's the first pheasant I ever bagged. I shot it with my dad a few years ago. Anyway, our neighbors put a floodlight on their garage. They said it was for security, but I think maybe they had other reasons."

I didn't say anything. One thing I'd figured out was that Gary was going to say what he was going to say, even if you weren't interested in hearing it.

He went on, "That floodlight made my pheasant throw a distorted shadow on the wall, all bent out of shape. For all practical purposes, it ruined my pheasant."

"Are you saying your neighbor did it on purpose?"

"Not for certain. I'm just saying it's possible. I've had bad vibes from him before."

"You burned down the garage to get the light turned off."

"Not at first. At first I tried to pry the floodlight off the garage with a crowbar. It didn't work because the light was wired up in conduit. In case you don't know, that's a heavy electrical pipe. Also, there were strong metal clamps."

"Why didn't you just move your pheasant to a different wall or close your curtains?"

"You sound just like Mrs. Greene," he said. "You sound just like everybody else who hears about the pheasant. The answer should be obvious: Why should I move my pheasant, when it was on the wall long before he put up his stupid floodlight?"

I didn't try to think of an answer. You couldn't give Gary a right answer; he made up all the rules for the conversation and if you broke one of the rules, he would go into this real injured head. I picked up my book again and started reading. I guess he got the point because he left and went down the hallway.

The Elms was squeezing me. As soon as he was out of sight, I went down to Mrs. Greene's office. Her secretary told me I'd have to wait, so I took a seat. I got to thinking that maybe I'd been jerked around long enough. The best thing for me would be to pack my few essential belongings, get on the road, and make my way to the reservation, where I could fulfill my true destiny as a Sioux.

It would be almost impossible to find me. There

were several people, including Barb, who would expect me to head for an Indian reservation, but their problem would be, which one? There are hundreds of reservations, all the way from the East Coast to the West Coast. In the state of Oklahoma there are more than thirty reservations, and in California, more than seventy.

The secretary broke my train of thought when she told me I could talk to Mrs. Greene now.

The first thing I told her was, I wouldn't take Gary for a roommate any more.

"Does Gary scare you?" asked Mrs. Greene.

"I'll sleep in the lounge," I said. "Or I'll sleep in the hall, but I won't be with him."

"I asked you if Gary scares you."

"Of course he scares me. *Everybody* scares me here. *You* scare me. I don't belong here, and it can't be good for me to be here." *But what was the alternative*, I asked myself, *back to Gates House?*

Mrs. Greene was opening up a folder. "Floyd, I've tried to tell you you won't be here for very long. Only a few days at the most."

"Yeah, but what does a few days mean?"

"I can't be more specific. In the meantime, I'll see what I can do about getting you transferred to another room."

She had her glasses on by this time, and I guess she found the papers she was looking for, because she closed up the folder. "Floyd, would you tell me about the X on the floor?"

"That's not why I came here."

"I know, but would you please tell me anyway?"

I sighed. "Mrs. Grice put an X on the floor of the lounge. She made people stand on it for punishment. Sometimes she made people stand on it for an hour or two."

"It says here you removed the X from the floor several times."

"That's true."

"Did she know who was removing the X?"

"No. I was doing it in the middle of the night. She figured it was me, but she didn't *know*."

"Did Mrs. Grice ever make you stand on the X?"

"She tried to make me once, but I refused."

"Floyd, why were you taking the X off the floor?"

"It was the principle of the thing. She kept giving people punishment they didn't deserve, and standing on the X was too embarrassing. I'd say the best word would be humiliating."

Mrs. Greene said, "Why do you think Mrs. Grice used that method of punishment?"

"Probably your basic power trip. I don't know why Mrs. Grice does the things she does. Why don't you ask her? As a matter of fact, if you want people in The Elms for observation, I'd say she'd be a good one to start with."

"And yet," said Mrs. Greene, "she's not the only authority figure you seem to have difficulties with." By this time, she was looking at a different set of papers. She changed the subject and started summarizing some of my test results. There was nothing wrong with me physically, but she said my mental tests showed that I was a loner. She asked me if I thought it was true.

"I suppose it is," I said. "Does it mean there's something the matter with me?"

"No, it doesn't. I'm just interested. You like activities you can do alone. Have you ever had what you would call a close friend?"

All of a sudden I got real uptight with her, and real impatient. She kept asking me these obvious things in this real nitpicky way, like she was trying to chip away at something. I thought about Gary's theory that all these things were a trap, but thinking about him only made me more impatient.

"I think I know what you're getting at," I said. "So let me sum it up. I've been moved around so many times that I've never had what you would call a basic circle of friends. I've never been in the same school more than two years in a row. I don't know my father or my mother, so if I have any relatives, I don't know who they are. Since you've got my files, I'm sure you know all of this. My way of making up for it is doing things by myself, such as reading and writing. I would say it's only logical."

Either Mrs. Greene didn't care for my attitude, or she had other things to deal with. She said, "We can talk more about this later. Was there anything else you wanted?"

"Yeah," I said. "Can I have my pipe back?"

"Your pipe?"

"My ceremonial Dakota pipe. It got confiscated.

Since it's one of my most prized possessions, I'd like it back."

Now she knew what I was talking about. "I think we're finished with it," she said. "I'll ask one of the nurses to put it in your bolster."

"Thank you." That was like a sign. When I left her office, my decision was made: I was taking off. There was no other way. Even if Barb worked her head off to get me the best placement, no one would listen to her; you had to admire her feistiness, but it was because of the feistiness that she would end up getting hung out, just like me.

In group therapy, everything got waylaid when Gary got into a long argument with a patient named Mr. Horderne. I don't know what the fight was about, but it gave me time to think about making a break. The doors at The Elms weren't locked, but you couldn't just walk out without permission; I would have to find a way to sneak out with nobody seeing me.

After supper, I went to the lounge and opened up a magazine. I wasn't really reading it, though, I was watching this supply closet down the hall where an orderly was going in and out. It was somewhat tense watching him, but then he finally made a trip clear down to the other end of the hall. The closet door was open.

As quick as I could, I popped inside the closet. I opened all the drawers of a cabinet until I found one with hand tools, tape, extension cords, et cetera. There were several screwdrivers, so I took the largest one. I put it in the back pocket of my blue jeans and pulled my shirttail down to cover it. Then I closed up the drawers and peeked out to scope the hallway; no one was coming, but my heart was pounding a mile a minute.

I went back to my seat in the lounge, just like nothing ever happened, and opened my magazine. I hoped my outside appearance was calm, but I was real shaky on the inside, and the screwdriver was cutting into my back.

Lights were out at ten-thirty on our wing. I was in bed, but wide awake and with my clothes on. I was waiting until eleven o'clock when there was a change of shift; the night nurses would come in and do some talking with the other nurses, who were getting ready to leave. If nobody did a room check right away, I could be gone a couple of hours or more before anybody knew I was missing.

About ten minutes to eleven, I heard some night staff coming in, and I could hear some gabbing and laughing down the hall at the nurses' station. I got out of bed and pulled the screwdriver out from under the pillow. Gary was snoring away; he was a sound sleeper and besides that, he was on some heavy-duty medication.

You were allowed to have the door to your room closed, so I pushed it, but I was careful not to slam it. Then I slid the screwdriver in between the two doors of the bolster, right where the lock was. I popped it hard, and it broke open with a loud crack.

Gary turned over in bed and lifted his head. "What the hell was that?"

"Nothing, I just crashed into the cabinet."

"Why are you out of bed?"

"Had to go to the john. Sorry." My heart was pounding away again. I only hoped to God they hadn't heard the crack down the hall.

Then Gary rolled back the other way. As far as I could tell, he was back to sleep. Anyway, he was quiet. I just stood there for a minute or two, taking deep breaths and trying to get my nerves and my pulse slowed down. Nobody came to our room.

I opened the cabinet door; there was enough light from the bathroom that I could see okay. Right next to my backpack was my ceremonial. I picked it up and held it. It was the final sign; if I needed one last piece of evidence that I was making the right decision, this was it. I was steady. All of a sudden, my nerves were like a rock.

I stuffed everything in the backpack, even the pipe, although it stuck out somewhat. I peeked out to check the halls; the nurses were yukking it up at their station, probably swapping a few stories about the weirdos they worked with. What did I care, I had a date with my destiny.

It was only a few steps down the hall to the exit door; I slipped through and made sure it was quiet when I closed it. The stairway was easy; institutional stairways are run by fire codes, so they're real private. I had to go down two flights. The exit door at the bottom took me out into the parking lot, where

I had to be careful; there was lots of light and I had to watch out for security personnel.

I got across the street as quickly as I could, onto this residential sidewalk with lots of old trees. It was dark and safe and private.

The walk to Barb's house took me forty minutes. It was only a couple of miles, so I could have made it faster, but I was keeping to the side streets to avoid public places with serious lighting. I approached her house from the back, by way of the alley; I had to be alert, in case any cops were cruising the neighborhood.

Her garage wasn't locked; it was only pegged with a dowel shoved down through the hasp. I slipped inside and pulled the door shut behind me. I laid a quarter-inch sheet of plywood up in front of the one window so I could turn on a trouble light without it being seen from the outside. Then I went to work on Nicky's Kawasaki.

I didn't give it the kind of attention it deserved, but then I didn't exactly have a lot of time to spare. I cleaned the fuel filters and the fuel lines, I cleaned the points and set the gap. I had to pump up the back tire. With the pressure to work fast, and being in the closed-up garage, I was sweating like a dog. I took five or six essential hand tools from the workbench so I'd have a basic tool kit to take with me on the road. Using the gas from the lawn mower can, I made sure the tank was full.

I didn't feel proud of the fact that I was about to take Nicky's motorcycle, but I was in this real get-on-with-it head. I knew that I was taking off, I knew how to go about it, and I wasn't in the mood for a lot of reflecting on right and wrong or consequences. Besides, he never paid any money for the bike, and he never took the time to work on it himself. Not only that, I planned to ship it back to him from the reservation, in much better shape than it was now.

I got the house key from the nail and went in Barb's house through the back door. After I drank about a gallon of water from the sink, I took half a loaf of bread and a half-full bottle of apple juice from the refrigerator and wedged them inside the backpack.

I wrote out a long note to Barb. I told her I was only taking off because they were about to hang me out again, and I hoped she would understand and not hold it against me. I told her not to worry because I was only going home to my destiny.

I left the note on the fireplace mantel. It ended up next to the picture of her son, who was dead, and her husband, also dead. I got some wholesale guilt out of this. In fact, this was the point where I almost lost my nerve. But instead of chickening out, I was inspired to write a P.S.:

> I just want you to know how much I appreciate all you tried to do for me, especially the log. You are a very quality person.
>
> Signed, CBC

By the time I went out the back door, it was a little past two-thirty in the A.M. I stood in the yard for a few moments looking at the log, but then I began to feel the guilt again. I got the motorcycle out of the garage and closed the door.

I walked the bike about three blocks to the Clark gas station. There was nobody at the gas station, of course, and all the streets were totally silent. I sat on the bike and got ready to fire it up. The first two times I kicked down on it, nothing happened. I got a sliver of panic. I felt real conspicuous, but it was too late to think about turning back. The bike *had* to start.

It started on the third try.

I got out of town as fast as I could and headed straight north on a country blacktop. It didn't take long for my eyes to get used to the dark. The cornfields whizzed by.

I could have been uptight about a lot of things, if I wanted to. The bike wasn't reliable, I was driving with no license, there was no headlight, I might run into a county lawman, and so on. The Pine Ridge Reservation was 800 miles away and I only had forty dollars in my pocket.

But I wasn't uptight at all; in fact, I was the opposite, which I guess would be ecstatic. I was free, like a bird, with the current carrying me. I was Charly Black Crow, and destiny was just ahead.

CHAPTER NINE

The fourth day of my *hanblecheya* was amazing. I went into a completely new mental zone, where all my emotions were numb; I didn't care what happened to me, but I didn't *not* care, either. I was awake, but I wasn't thinking; my mind was like a receiver.

Maybe it was from being so hungry and so tired. Maybe that was the idea of the *hanblecheya*, to break you down, so you were ready to receive your vision. Anyway, I just sat there like a stone, more or less. I saw pictures without thinking; my brain was like a screen for somebody's slide show. This was not a head I tried to get into; trying had nothing to do with it.

I crawled out of the cave and up on top of the mound, where I just eased down into the pine-needle carpet. It was almost like I wasn't there, I was just part of what was already there. I don't think words can really describe it.

I saw the Stone Boy legend complete. The pictures just came into my brain, real slow, one after another. I couldn't tell if I was watching him or if I was inside of him.

Stone Boy tracked his ancestors to the savage hunting ground of *Iya*, the Evil One. The Evil One sent showers of boulders, but Stone Boy dodged them all. Then the thundering herds of the Buffalo People came, but Stone Boy ran them into the sea, where they drowned.

Then *Iya* took the form of the ferocious serpent tree. Every limb was a huge serpent. Stone Boy hacked away serpents with his spear, but new ones grew in their place. Bigger ones, and more of them.

Stone Boy limped back to the hovel of Old Woman, who gave him food and shelter. She gave him a small, broken mirror and told him to take it with him to fight *Iya*. But Stone Boy laughed; he had a strong shield and a sharp spear. What good would it do to have a mirror?

The next day he cut away more serpents, but again they grew back. And the day after, the same. Stone Boy realized that destroying the serpent tree meant more than destroying something *Iya* sent; it meant destroying the Evil One himself. Understanding this made him very discouraged. He couldn't deal with defeat because he was used to the successes that come to a hero.

That night, Old Woman said again, take the mirror. So he did. He went the next morning to the serpent tree, carrying the mirror. He held it up to the tree and one of the serpents devoured itself; it shriveled down into a small, dead twig. Then another, and another. Stone Boy danced around the huge tree, holding up the mirror; he watched one serpent after another devour itself until the whole tree was only a small, dead stump.

It was amazing. Stone Boy laughed. With *Iya* destroyed, all the ancestors returned to life. They rose from the dead, and there was a huge celebration.

The same pictures of the Stone Boy legend kept passing across my brain, in the same order. The pictures were clear and consistent.

After that, I guess I went to sleep. Or half asleep, maybe dozing in and out. I kept having these dreams about the Stone Boy sequence, only everything was distorted. The serpent tree was now *The System*, and the serpent faces were replaced by the faces of Mrs. Grice, Mrs. Bluefish, Mr. Saberhagen, Mrs. Greene, and Mr. Wagner.

I kept rolling over, awake and asleep. I wanted to wake up for good, but I didn't have the strength. The dream was nasty, and I didn't want it. Stone Boy hacked away the serpent head of Mrs. Lacey, but Mrs. Greene grew in its place. All their faces and you couldn't cut them out, no matter how hard you tried. I had this terrible headache and I wanted to wake up because the dream was bad; but I couldn't stay awake and I couldn't sleep in peace.

I don't know how long it went on. When I finally came to, I was back in the cave, right at the mouth; I didn't remember going in there, though. Donny Thunderbird was holding my arm, and I could smell burning sage. Since Donny was crouching right at the cave's entrance, he was mostly a silhouette, with bright blue sky behind him.

He was asking me if I was okay and could I sit up. When I finally did sit up, he helped me scoot out into the light. I was so weak, I felt like a baby; I was all plastered with sweat. I could hear Delbert Bear's chanting voice. I couldn't see him, but I knew he was up on top, burning sage and chanting to *Wakan Tanka*.

Donny had some soupy mash in a thermos. It was mostly rice, with little scraps of chicken mixed in. I ate six or eight spoonfuls. It tasted delicious, but it gave me a low-level stomachache. Then he gave me a thermos of tea, which was lukewarm, about room temperature.

"I wish it was iced tea," I said.

"A drink with ice in it would be bad for you. It would give you a headache." He was rummaging in my backpack. He got out my blue jeans.

"If you feel like you're up to it," he said, "I'll help you put these on."

I remembered I was naked. "I'm up to it," I said. Then I had my pants on.

He gave me some more to eat, but slowly. He told me I should be real proud for lasting the whole four days. The food was delicious, but it was giving me this warm, dizzy feeling. I guess it might have been a little like getting drunk, but I've never been drunk, so I really wouldn't know.

I probably had another half pint of the food before Donny took it away. Then I drank some more of the tea. I asked him if we were going back now and he said, "Not yet; you're not ready."

"Are we going back to the sweat lodge?"

"Not the sweat lodge. We'll go back to the tipi in the village."

"Your sister will be there," I said.

"Right. She'll give you some more of this gruel, if you feel up to it."

"How soon are we going?"

"There's no hurry. Delbert has a lot more sage to burn." While Donny was talking to me, he was gazing out across the hills. You could see so far. I wondered what he was thinking about.

After about half an hour, we walked all the way down to the village. It took a long time because being real shaky on my feet, I had to stop and rest every once in a while. Donny helped me walk, but Delbert wasn't much help at all. Besides being a little drunk, he was mostly interested in doing the chanting and burning the sage.

When we finally made it to the tipi, Donny's sister gave me some chicken soup. She said to me, "Congratulations."

I told her thank you, though I wasn't sure if that was the right thing to say. I took a long time eating the soup, and I also drank a lot of water. I was feeling a lot better, but still somewhat shaky.

After that, Donny drove me down the mountain in the pickup truck. He took me on down to that tipi in the campground where I started out the first night. He asked me if I needed anything but I told him no, I would be fine. Exhausted, I fell asleep in the tipi.

It must have been a long nap because the sun was low when I woke up. I walked over to the shower house and scrubbed down under a hot shower, working up about a ton of lather. During my soap-down, I started thinking about the vision quest. It could have bummed me out, though, and the shower was making me feel like a new man; I managed to put the thoughts out of my mind.

After that, I did my laundry in this Laundromat up by the tourist shops. I was real hungry. While my clothes were in the machine, I bought two Kit Kat bars and a Pepsi. I sat on the porch in front of the building, munching and drinking. I was beginning to feel my stomach returning. Even though it was getting dark, lots of tourists were milling around. After being on the *hanblecheya* for four days, it was sort of nice having people around, but I was glad I didn't have to talk to any of them.

When all my clothes were done in the dryer, I went back to the tipi and folded them up neatly in my backpack. I sat on the riverbank for a while, watching the stars come out and feeling numb; it was a mystical kind of feeling, which lasted quite a while. It was bittersweet, I guess you might say.

I had a good night's sleep in the tipi, with no tossing and turning and no dreams.

I got up early the next day. It was a beautiful, clear morning, slightly cooler. I went around for a while picking up litter in the campground, such as

Pepsi cans and cigarette packs. Could you believe these slobs who couldn't even control themselves in a place of such natural beauty?

I threw all the trash in a barrel and went up to the coffee shop, where I bought a Styrofoam cup of coffee and a jelly donut. Then I walked back down to the riverbank. The gooey food tasted great, but I hardly had time to finish it before Donny came by in the pickup. He said the chief wanted to talk to me now. "He wants to interpret your vision," Donny said.

The interpretation of the *hanblecheya* led by a tribal elder is the final part of a vision quest. This had to be a moment of high honor: The chief himself was going to act as my interpreter.

Donny asked me, "Are you ready?"

I didn't feel like I was, not really, but this was the chief calling. "I guess I'd better be," I said. Then I added, "I need to get my backpack first."

When we got to the trailer, Chief Bear-in-cave greeted me at the door. He asked me if I was feeling well enough to have a little talk. I said sure.

We would be sitting at the kitchen table again. He got down to search for something in a low cupboard. You could see him wince a little bit. Maybe it was pain from arthritis or some kind of injury, but the thing you knew for sure was, he wouldn't complain.

It turned out what he was rummaging around for was a leather pouch, which he put on the table. Before he took his own seat, he asked me if I cared for some tea. I told him no thanks. He congratulated me for sticking out the whole *hanblecheya*. "I think you are a young man of honor," he said. "I thought so on the first day we talked."

I felt proud, but I couldn't think of anything to say to that. Then the chief picked up the pouch and he asked me, "Do you have your Dakota pipe?"

"It's in my backpack," I told him.

"We should smoke it now."

I got out the pipe and handed it over. Chief Bear-in-cave fingered it and eyeballed it from his good side. I guess he approved of it, because he started packing the bowl. He lit it up and puffed a few times to get it going, then passed it over. As he did, he told me if I had a vision, he would like to hear about it.

I took a drag; I don't know what we were smoking, but it sure wasn't willow bark. I started by telling him, "I almost quit on the second day. I almost gave up and came back down."

"Let's hear about it," he said.

So I summed up the bad day when I figured out my "destiny" was more or less phony.

"Why do you say phony?"

"Because it's like a mind game. I've been using the destiny to try and make up for several years of getting jerked around."

The chief didn't say anything right away. He shook his head, then walked slowly across to the stove to pour himself a cup of tea. When he got back into his seat, he shook his head again and passed me the pipe. "Perhaps there's nothing wrong at all with your destiny. Perhaps the only wrong is wanting it all at once."

I asked him to explain.

"Trying to grab a destiny is like trying to grab water from the river with your fist. It doesn't work. Do you understand?"

"Not completely," I admitted.

"The grand thing about a destiny is that you learn it bit by bit, the way you learn a river. You love the Dakota and the values of the Dakota. You might say that's how the destiny begins. That's what puts you on the river, in your boat. Right now, you understand only part of your destiny. The rest will come to you."

"But how will I know the rest?"

"By letting it come to you. By not trying to grab it. Four days ago, you quoted Black Elk to me, now I will quote Black Elk to you." He broke into one of his wide, toothless grins. "Black Elk says, 'Make your mind clear and open like the big sky.' You have a set of values, now let your destiny unfold."

It was plenty to think about. But from us doing so much talking, the pipe was out; the chief was lighting it with a match. He said, "What you've just told me about is not a vision. To use your word, it's a funk." He was all of a sudden laughing and slapping his knee.

It was altogether funny, just looking and listening to his style. I couldn't help laughing, too.

He regrouped and said, "I don't know what a funk is, but I'm sure it's not a vision."

When I was done laughing I said, "I think maybe the last few hours was the vision." I told him about the mental zone I went into and the clear pictures of the Stone Boy legend that came to me.

The chief listened real carefully to the whole thing. When I was finished he said, "Stone Boy defeated *Iya* by using the mirror given to him by Old Woman."

"That's the way it came out," I said.

"And some day soon you'll write it all down." It didn't sound like a question, but I knew it was.

"Sure I will," I answered. "It's what I do best."

"I'll tell you this much," said the chief. "It's the best Stone Boy tale I've ever heard." Naturally, this remark made me proud.

"I've been working on the Stone Boy legend a long time," I told him.

"And yet you saw it complete when you didn't work on it at all. When you let it come to you."

"That's true," I said. It wasn't hard to see what he was getting at.

Apparently the chief felt we needed to smoke another bowl, because he was repacking and relighting. "This sounds like the real thing, doesn't it?" he said.

"I guess so."

"You were Stone Boy?"

"I felt like I was. I had a dream about it afterward. It was more like a nightmare because I couldn't wake up to make it stop. The serpent tree, *Iya*, was the system of social workers and specialists. Houseparents and psychologists. Their faces were like the serpent branches, and they couldn't be destroyed."

"The system is a monster."

"It's like a monster, with a life of its own. It just jerks you around and runs your life. You don't have any control of your own life, the system has it all."

The chief took a long drag. He said, "Yet Stone Boy did have the power, did he not?"

At this point I looked down. "It's true. He had the power when he trusted Old Woman."

The phone rang then. It was a wall phone in the kitchen, so it was on the fourth ring before the chief, still moving slowly, got there. He said "Yes" into the receiver, then he didn't say anything at all for about sixty seconds. When he said "Yes" the second time, he hung up.

He came back with his index finger raised. "I have this thought," he said. "Because of his miraculous birth, Stone Boy was half stone, but not *all* stone. The other half was flesh."

"In other words, the other half was human."

"Mmmm. Tell me something. The serpent tree is the system that has troubled your life. But who is Old Woman?"

I didn't even have to think, I just blurted it out: "Old Woman is Barb. My social worker."

The chief didn't say anything, he just nodded his head a few times.

After a pause I said, "You're saying I need to put my trust in her."

"Is it what I'm saying, or what you're saying?"

"I'm the one who had the vision, so I guess I'm the one saying it. When Stone Boy stopped fighting on his own and put his trust in Old Woman, that's when he finally succeeded."

After that, we were quiet for a long, long time. In fact, we didn't say anything for all the time it took to smoke the rest of the pipe. I was real happy about sticking out the *hanblecheya*, and having an authentic vision, and having Chief Bear-in-cave there to help me interpret. But I had the downside also, because I could see the conclusion we were headed for, though we weren't saying it out loud.

Finally the chief said, "Would you like to talk to your social worker?"

"Barb? Is she here?"

"She's not here now. But she's on the way."

"She is? When is she coming?"

"I'm not sure. I talked to her on the phone. She said she would come as soon as she could."

That was a thought. She was driving up herself. She could have just notified the local cops to take me back. "I think I'd like to talk to her," I said.

"That would be a good thing," the chief agreed.

When I left the chief's trailer, I walked to the mechanic shop, hoping to find Donny. I had an idea. I was in luck: I found him sharpening some mower blades.

He asked me how my session with the chief went.

"Good," I said. "He gave me a lot of food for thought. To tell you the truth, though, I can't get it out of my head that this was a screwup."

"How so?"

"Taking off like I did, to become an Indian. Stealing Nicky's bike, leaving Barb in the lurch. You know what I mean?"

"Don't be too hard on yourself. If somebody put me in the looney bin, I'd probably do the same thing. Or maybe even something worse."

"It wasn't just the looney bin. That was what you'd call the last straw. I feel real bad about taking Nicky's bike. Even though he didn't take care of it, it's still his." Then I wondered when Barb was coming. Chief Bear-in-cave only said she was coming; he hadn't said when. Without any warning, I found myself anxious to see her.

Donny said, "Don't forget, you completed the *hanblecheya.* Something good always comes from that."

I couldn't argue with him. I couldn't be negative about one of the most honored traditions of Dakota life.

Donny changed the subject. "I have to drive to town to get some stuff; would you like to go with me?"

This got my attention. "Is there a parts store?"

"Yeah. Why?"

"I'd like to work on Nicky's bike. I don't know if I can fix it, but I'd like to try."

"Let's go for it."

I didn't pay too much attention to the town itself when we got there, I was more interested in getting what I needed and taking care of business. Before we went to the parts store, we had to take care of Donny's errands. That meant rounding up a case of garbage bags, a couple cases of toilet paper, some cleaning supplies, and even a little bit of lumber.

Afterward, I was able to get a headlight for the bike, which cost $22.50. I also bought six cans of Pennzoil and a can of rubbing compound. My funds were suddenly down to six bucks, but I didn't want to think about that.

CHAPTER TEN

When we got back to the reservation, it was way past noon. We went right to the equipment shed where I helped Donny unload his stuff. He told me he had work to do, so he couldn't help me with the bike. But I said that was okay because I needed to try and psych it out on my own anyway.

Then he left. I was the only person in the shop, which suited me just fine. I pulled the Kawasaki over by the workbench, where all the tools were kept and the light was good.

I don't really have enough mechanical know-how to fix a seized-up engine, but I wanted to try a trick I saw Mr. Gibbs use once on a seized-up Rototiller. He took the head off and poured small amounts of oil on top of the piston, so it could seep down into the cylinder walls. I didn't know of anything better to try, and all the sockets and other tools I needed were right on the workbench. I could only hope and pray that the engine damage wasn't too severe.

To get at the head, I had to take off the gas tank, both carburetors, the sediment bowl, and the exhaust pipes. It took a long time, partly because I was stopping to clean everything as I went. I may not be an expert mechanic, but when it comes to engines, I know dirt is the enemy.

I was just picking the sockets I'd need to take off the head when a voice from behind startled me: "I'm looking for Charly Black Crow. Can you tell me where to find him?"

I turned around, and there was Barb. "I didn't hear you come in. How did you find the shop?"

"I asked for directions."

"Are you pissed at me?"

"I'm too tired for that. This has been a long drive. Is there a chair anywhere around here?"

I found her a chair, and she said she was thirsty. I got her a Pepsi from a pop machine around back. As embarrassed as I was about my escapade, I found I was real glad to see her.

She leaned back in her chair and drank some of the Pepsi. She said, "This is a long way from home, but it looks familiar. You're working on Nicky's bike and up to your elbows in grease."

"It's got a seized-up engine. I'm trying to fix it."

"That sounds serious."

"It seized up on the highway. It was burning oil, only I didn't see it because I was driving in the dark."

"Can you fix it?"

"Maybe. I really hope so. I feel real guilty about stealing Nicky's bike. The thing is, when he gets it back, it has to be in better shape than before; that won't square everything, but it would be a start."

While we were talking, I started taking out the bolts holding down the head. They were rusted tight, so I had to use some Liquid-Wrench. "You came by yourself," I said to her.

"I came by myself."

"Does the agency know where I am?"

"No. They're networking, but you picked an awfully good hiding place. When your chief called, I just decided to see if I could deal with it on my own."

"You·went out on a limb for me."

"We could call it that, I suppose. I'd say your chief did, too. There are people who are willing to go to bat for you, Floyd."

"That's true about the chief," I said. She had a good point.

Then she said, "What's a *hanblecheya*?"

"It's a vision quest," I said. I went ahead and summed up the history and purpose of the *hanblecheya*.

"You were out in the wilderness for four days and nights with nothing to eat?"

"That's the way it's done."

"I really admire you for it. It had to take a lot of courage."

"I needed to see it through," I said. "Not only for the meaning of it, but also because the chief was treating me with such high honor, when he could've just turned me over to the cops for a runaway."

By this time the head was off, and I poured about a pint of oil on top of each piston. I sat up on the workbench next to Barb. We hadn't talked about my going back; I couldn't yet.

"Now what?" she said.

"We have to wait a few minutes." You could see some of the oil dripping on the floor, but it looked like most of it was working its way down inside the cylinders.

I guess the gods were with us, because it worked. The oil penetrated, and both cylinders were freed up. I blew out a sigh of relief.

"Success?" Barb asked.

"I think so. Keep your fingers crossed." I poured a little more oil on top of both sides, then I brought the engine oil up to the right level. Then I went to work putting the whole bike back together. When that was finished, I looked over at Barb, but she was sound asleep in her chair. Her fingers were crossed.

Since she was sleeping, I gave the bike a good workout with the rubbing compound. It shined up pretty good, considering its age and all the neglect it had suffered.

I pushed it out of the shop, quite a distance away so I wouldn't wake her up when I started it. It was easy starting. I took it out on the road for a test run. All things considered it was running pretty well, but you could see the blue smoke coming out. It would never be a good-running bike without new rings. If you rode it any distance, you'd have to carry oil with you so you could add some every now and then.

When I got back from the test run, Barb was awake. "I see you got it running," she said.

"Yeah, plus it looks a lot better, don't you think?"

"It looks nice, Floyd. It looks so much better, I hardly recognize it."

"This'll make Nicky happy."

"I know it will," she said. Then she changed the subject. "Floyd, I'm about to starve. Didn't I see a coffee shop or something over by those tourist shops?"

"There're places to eat. Let's go over."

When we got to the coffee shop, Barb ordered two double cheeseburgers. I told her she must be real hungry.

"One of them's for you," she said.

"But I'm broke."

"Not anymore, you're not. I brought you some money."

"Your money or mine?" I asked.

"Yours. I took it from your account."

"Well, I am sort of hungry."

"Good." She lit up a cigarette while we were waiting for our food. I told her I'd like to see her give up smoking.

"I'm working on it," she said. "Now let me tell you what I'd like you to do."

I told her I was listening.

"I've had a couple of talks with Wagner and Lacey this week. They've agreed to drop all the talk about moving you to another group home."

She was talking about my going back.

She went on, "I have two possible placements in private homes that I think you might like. They're both right in town. You can meet the people, if you want, and then it would be up to you. Nobody would force you."

"You're talking about me going back."

"And one other thing. No probation. If you go back to Gates House, you won't be on probation."

"But you're talking about me going back. Don't ask me that now."

"Okay, I'm listening," she said.

"I'm trying to tell you this is a real mixed bag. The *hanblecheya* was real meaningful and important, and I'm glad the bike is fixed. But this whole thing was probably a screwup, and I'm still in somewhat of a funk. I'm just not ready to talk about going back."

"You took off because you felt trapped. You couldn't see any other way out. People in that situation sometimes do extreme things."

"And that's another thing. You're not like the system. I don't know how you're getting away with stuff."

"Getting away with what stuff? Other than coming up here on my own, and not telling anybody where you are, all I've been doing is speaking up for what I believe in."

"That's not the way it works," I said.

"That's the way *I* work. I'm like the flies at the picnic, I won't go away. I think the powers that be are starting to realize it. I can't be fired for standing up for my beliefs, even if I do it in no uncertain terms."

You had to respect her point of view, but she was talking about the system. Then we didn't have to talk about it anymore, because the cheeseburgers came.

When we were finished eating, it was almost six o'clock. Since there were a couple hours of daylight left, Barb wanted to know if I would show her some of the reservation.

"I can show you the parts I know about," I said.

We went in her old station wagon. I gave her directions that put us on that same rough road Donny and I followed the first day of my vision seek. Barb kept asking me was I serious, but I kept telling her the drive would be worth it.

Eventually we got to Donny's village and came to a stop. She checked it out and said, "I had no idea places like this still existed."

"It's a kick, isn't it? This is the real thing, Barb." I told her if we went a mile or two farther, we would be able to see Mount Black Elk.

"What's Mount Black Elk?"

"That's my name for the place where I had the *hanblecheya*. We won't be close to it, but we'll be able to see it."

"Why not?" she said. She started up the car. We went as far as we could, but the road was so primitive, it was like it wasn't there anymore.

She stopped the car and said, "I'm afraid this is as far as we go."

"It's far enough," I said. We got out of the car and sat on the front fender. You could see the mountaintop, just barely, but it was too far away to make out the cave or the pine trees. The sun was very low in the west, which gave the peak a sort of mystical golden glow.

"You were up there four days and nights by yourself, without a bite to eat."

"It doesn't seem possible now, not with all this food in my stomach and all the sleep I got last night."

"Why do you call it Mount Black Elk?"

"There's a legend that it was Black Elk's favorite place to go on a *hanblecheya*."

"It's very beautiful," she said. "Your view from up there must have been majestic."

"I'd say that's a good word for it." Then we just looked at the peak in the late sun for a long time, without talking. It was good memories and a mellowed-out feeling, especially with Barb there to share it.

After a long silence I finally said to her, "I have to go back, don't I?"

"My late husband, God rest his soul, always said the only things we have to do are die and pay taxes."

"But you know what I'm saying. Even though I'll feel like a fool."

Barb said, "There doesn't seem to be another right choice, now that you mention it."

"Dakota wisdom says if you're in touch with your inner voice, you know when it's time to do a thing. Even dying; you know when it's time for that."

"What is your inner voice saying?"

"I already told you. There's one thing, though. If I go back, I have to drive the bike."

"Do you have a license?"

"You can't get a license until you're sixteen."

She looked at me and went into a sort of hesitation. "I'm already out on the limb pretty far," she said. "You want me to crawl clear out to the tip and break it off?"

"I know it's asking a lot. But it's important to me; I'm the one who stole it and I have to be the one who takes it back."

"Better than it was?" she asked.

"Right. I have to take it back in better shape than it was. It would feel like I was getting a little honor back."

"I'll offer a compromise," she said. "We'll go back together. You drive the bike, and I'll follow behind in the car. How's that?"

I thought about it. It might be an advantage to have the car along; we could store extra quarts of engine oil in the back. And I would still be driving the bike back.

"That could be okay," I said.

On the drive back down, I asked her if she'd like to spend the night in my tipi.

"Not likely. I'm too old for that. I've got a room at a motel in town."

When she dropped me off in the campground, it was almost dark. She said she'd see me for breakfast.

She didn't add that we'd have to reach a firm decision about her travel compromise, but she didn't have to.

By the next morning I was in the right head. We were eating breakfast in the coffee shop when I said to Barb, "I'll go ahead and meet the two foster placements."

"I'll arrange it so you can. It will be your decision, though."

"I understand."

"If you don't feel comfortable about either one, then we'll see if we can find some other options."

"I understand." I ate some more of my sausage, gravy, and biscuits. Then I asked her if I'd ever told her about the Stone Boy legend.

"I think you mentioned it once or twice, but not in detail."

"That was the most important part of the *hanble-cheya*," I told her. "The legend came to me complete. It also got very symbolic, which is where the chief came in; he helped me interpret." I went ahead to explain to her the connection between Stone Boy's legend and certain parts of my own life.

"You are Old Woman," I told her.

"Great." she said. "I've been called Coarse Woman for years, now I get to be Old Woman."

"That's not the point," I said. "It's what these things stand for. Stone Boy was half stone, but also half flesh. When he put his trust in Old Woman, his human side came out."

"This was your vision," she said.

"That's the vision. I have to put my trust in you, and I think I can do it. I have to change my thinking. Belonging is important to me, but you can't really do it until you're ready to belong."

Not that these things were easy for me to say to her; in fact, it was embarrassing. But when a thing needs to be said, you have to find a way. Barb didn't say anything. She was drinking her coffee and thinking.

I told her, "You said to me that I can't turn everything in, sometimes I have to turn out and ask for help."

"I said it and I believe it. But you were right, too, Floyd."

"How was I right?"

She said, "The social services system *is* something like the serpent tree in your Stone Boy legend. Big bureaucracies can get that way; they can turn into monsters. They get so they serve their own needs rather than the people they're supposed to help."

"I know. But if you never find a place to put your trust, it's like you turn to stone."

It wasn't too long after that when Barb said, "We've got a long trip ahead of us. We need to think about getting started."

"I've got my stuff packed. But I'd like to say good-bye to the chief before we go."

"No doubt you would. You think maybe I could meet him?"

We drove to the chief's trailer. We didn't have an

175

invitation, so I felt a little funny, just dropping in. But the chief was glad to see us.

I introduced him and Barb; the two of them shook hands and said how happy they were to meet each other. We all sat down at Chief Bear-in-cave's kitchen table, where he had a lot of papers and folders spread around.

He asked me, "Is it time to go?"

"Yeah," I said. "It's time. Let's be realistic, I can't pick up campground litter for the rest of my life. Besides, the *hanblecheya* has helped me get into a new head."

He smiled. "I was expecting you today. I thought it would be time."

"Why?" I asked.

He was still smiling. "Dakota wisdom," he said. "I'm glad you did come, because there are a couple of things for us to discuss."

I asked what they were.

"Item number one, I make you a suggestion. Next summer, why not come here and work on the reservation? We have summer staff jobs for teenagers. Unfortunately, all the jobs are filled for this year. The work would be monotonous and the pay would be low. But you would spend the summer living and working among the Dakota. It might take you around another bend or two on the river, which might teach you more about your destiny."

"Sign me up," I said, with no hesitation.

"Not so fast. Think it over and talk it over with this lady." He nodded in Barb's direction. "I think she is a good person who will not stand in the way of things that are beneficial to you."

"I can't tell you how much I appreciate this."

The chief held up his hand like a stop sign. "Now the second thought. Remember, I had two. I have something to show you. Please follow me."

Barb and I both followed him into the den part of the trailer. Chief Bear-in-cave put on his glasses. I wondered if the right side had a lens in it or just clear glass. Anyway, he got three ledger books from the bookshelves, and sat at a small desk nearby.

He said, "We keep records of everyone who is enrolled in the tribe. As you can see, our records are kept the old-fashioned way, in ledger books. The records aren't perfect, but I daresay they are more accurate than the records in the Bureau of Indian Affairs, even though they keep theirs in a computer."

Barb said, "The Bureau of Indian Affairs sounds like another one of those serpent trees that Floyd has nightmares about."

"Most definitely," said the chief. "A monster with many heads." He waved his arm at all the books on the shelves and continued, "We also have our history stored here. It isn't organized quite the way it ought to be, but it's all here if a person wants to take the time to find it."

He looked up at me and said, "You have said you want to be a Dakota. These are my thoughts about it. Years and years ago, it was easy to know who was a red man and who was a white man. For that matter, I suppose it was simple to know who was a black man, who was a Jew, and so on."

He got another book from the shelf. It wasn't a ledger book, it was one with a regular black binding. "Things are different now from what they were in the old days. It isn't easy now to identify Indians, as anyone who tries to take an Indian census knows. The government knows it better than anyone. This book is a publication of the Bureau of Indian Affairs." The chief stopped talking and started leafing through the pages, looking for a certain passage.

When he did find the passage, he read only a few sentences out loud: "In the eyes of the government, the identity of an 'Indian' is often blurred. If a man says he is an *Indian*, and can prove it, he is an *Indian*. To be counted as an Indian, a person must prove that he is an enrolled member of a tribe, band, or group recognized by the federal government."

Then he closed the book. He took off his glasses, looked at me out of the good eye, and said, "Do you understand?"

"I think so," I said. There was a lump in my stomach.

"A more folksy way of putting it would be, what a man is in his heart, that's he truly is. Anyhow, every enrolled member of this tribe pays twenty-five dollars a year to maintain his tribal status. It's sort of like paying dues. If you pay your twenty-five dollars, and I write your name in the tribal enrollment book, who is to say that you are not Dakota?"

"My money's low," I said quickly. "I'll have to

send you the twenty-five bucks after I get home."

"No you won't," said Barb. "Here's the money, right from your own account." She handed me the money, and I passed it over to the chief.

I felt really fulfilled and extremely warm inside. At that moment I felt so close to the one-eyed old chief and my social worker, I thought that maybe, if you knew your parents, and if you truly loved them, this might be something like how it would feel. There were tears forming in my eyes, but I had to blink them back, because I had a last request. Even so, it took a few moments.

Finally, I got enough composure and I said to Chief Bear-in-cave, "When you write my name in the book, please write Charly Black Crow, and not Floyd Rayfield."

The chief answered that if that's the way I wanted it, that's the way he would write it.

Before I left, Chief Bear-in-cave and I exchanged the Sioux embrace, gripping the backs of one another's upper arms. "I'll be seeing you next summer," I said.

The chief smiled, but he didn't speak.

EPILOGUE

Barb dropped me off at the shop so I could pick up the bike. I put the spare cans of Pennzoil in her car, along with my backpack. She left and said she'd meet me at the main gate.

I was in luck; Donny Thunderbird was in the shop, which gave me the chance to tell him good-bye. He helped me push the bike outside the shop. He said be sure and write, and I told him he could count on it.

"When you get your Stone Boy legend all written out, I'd like to have a copy of it," he said.

"Of course," I said. Real proud. I told him thanks for everything, and then the two of us exchanged the Sioux embrace.

Barb and I spent just a few minutes in one of the souvenir shops before we left. I bought a package of postcards, so I'd have some pictures of the reservation. Barb bought a copy of *Black Elk Speaks*. "I'll read this and then maybe I'll have some idea what this famous prophet was all about."

Then we went on out to the main parking lot. It was crowded with people and vehicles, just the way it was when I first saw it. I was about ready to climb on when Barb said, "This bike isn't even licensed, is it?"

I smiled at her. "The bike's not licensed and neither is the driver."

"Perfect. Is there anything else?"

I couldn't help laughing. "I don't have a helmet. That's against the law."

"I think I hear the limb cracking. If there's anything else, don't tell me."

"We'll only be on back roads. You don't attract much attention that way."

"Just don't lose me. And if we do get stopped by an officer, let me do the talking."

"You'd know what to say, wouldn't you?"

"Maybe yes, and maybe no. Let's hope we don't have to find out."

Then I climbed up onto the Kawasaki and fired it up. I headed on down the road with the wind whipping me in the face. The sky was big and blue; I had Barb's car in my rearview mirror. I felt real free.

I guess you could say there were a lot of loose ends. There were the placement interviews Barb was arranging, the baseball team back in Joliet, and the big log was probably still there, waiting to be finished. I wondered about coming back to the reservation in a year. I was hoping Nicky wouldn't be too pissed about the bike.

But mostly, I just thought about the one thing I was really sure of, and it gave me that peaceful, easy feeling: I was now an Indian.

About This Point Signature Author

James Bennett's first novel for young adults, *I Can Hear the Mourning Dove*, earned high praise from reviewers and was named an ALA Best Book for Young Adults. *Booklist* proclaimed it "powerful . . . unforgettable. . . ." It is currently available as a Scholastic Point paperback.

Mr. Bennett often finds his inspiration in the mentally handicapped students he works with as a teaching assistant at Bloomington High School. He lives in Normal, Illinois, with his wife and son, and is also the author of *A Quiet Desperation*, a nonfiction book for adults. *Dakota Dream* is James Bennett's first novel for Scholastic Hardcover.